He stared d
and sincere

She stamped
tried to be logi

"My gut is telling me you're innocent." His gaze went to the gun and then back to her face. "Relatively innocent."

A smile twitched her lips, and she felt the sudden, ridiculous urge to laugh at the predicament she'd gotten herself into. She'd never so much as gotten a parking ticket her whole life and in one day, she'd stolen a gun off one federal agent and taken another one hostage.

"Just level with me, Juliette," Andre said, his deep brown eyes imploring, almost hypnotizing in their intensity.

A shiver worked its way up her body that had nothing to do with fear. Letting her attraction for this man lull her into trusting him was a bad idea. Whether or not he believed her story, he was still a federal agent.

Dear Reader,

Thanks for joining me as The Lawmen series continues with The Lawmen: Bullets and Brawn miniseries. As children, Andre Diaz, Cole Walker and Marcos Costa formed their own family. Now these brothers try to unravel the secret that separated them so many years ago. The story begins with Andre, but watch for Cole's and Marcos's stories to hit shelves in the next two months.

If you missed the first miniseries, you can find out more about The Lawmen at my website, www.elizabethheiter.com. You can also learn more about my Profiler series from MIRA Books, and my FBI profiler Evelyn Baine, whose latest case involves the mysterious disappearance of a teenager who left behind a note foretelling her own death.

Thanks for reading! I hope you enjoy *Bodyguard with a Badge*!

Elizabeth Heiter

BODYGUARD WITH A BADGE

—

ELIZABETH HEITER

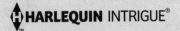
HARLEQUIN INTRIGUE®

For my amazing agent, Kevan Lyon. Thank you for believing in me.

Acknowledgments

Thank you to Paula Eykelhof, Denise Zaza, Kayla King and everyone involved in bringing *Bodyguard with a Badge* to shelves. Thanks to fellow Intrigue authors Barb Han, Janie Crouch and Tyler Anne Snell for #AllTheWords. And thanks to my family and friends for their endless support, with a special thanks to my usual suspects for their manuscript feedback and support: Chris Heiter, Robbie Terman, Andrew Gulli, Kathryn Merhar, Caroline Heiter, Kristen Kobet, Ann Forsaith, Charles Shipps, Sasha Orr, Nora Smith and Mark Nalbach.

ISBN-13: 978-0-373-75683-4

Bodyguard with a Badge

Copyright © 2017 by Elizabeth Heiter

Recycling programs for this product may not exist in your area.

HARLEQUIN®
www.Harlequin.com

Printed in U.S.A.

Elizabeth Heiter likes her suspense to feature strong heroines, chilling villains, psychological twists and a little romance. Her research has taken her into the minds of serial killers, through murder investigations and onto the FBI Academy's shooting range. Elizabeth graduated from the University of Michigan with a degree in English literature. She's a member of International Thriller Writers and Romance Writers of America. Visit Elizabeth at www.elizabethheiter.com.

CAST OF CHARACTERS

Andre Diaz—A sniper with the FBI's hostage rescue team, he's used to rescuing civilians, but when Juliette Lawson takes *him* hostage, he breaks all the rules to protect her. The problem is, her past is catching up to her fast. How can he find the truth when even her name is a lie?

Juliette Lawson—She's been on the run from her ex-husband for three years. When he finally catches up to her, she'll do whatever it takes to stay alive—including taking an FBI agent hostage. But as she falls for Andre, she realizes the only way to keep him safe may be to sacrifice herself.

Scott Delacorte—Andre's partner at the FBI. Scott thinks Andre is putting more than just his job at risk by hiding out with Juliette, but he's willing to cover for his partner as long as he can.

Cole Walker—Andre's older foster brother and a police detective. Cole instantly accepts Juliette because he can tell Andre is falling for her, but he's distracted by a new revelation about their past in the foster home.

Marcos Costa—Andre's younger foster brother and a DEA agent. Marcos can't reconcile the new theory Andre has about why they were all split up years ago in the foster system with what he remembers.

Dylan Keane—Juliette's ex-husband is also a police officer. It appears that he'll use any means necessary—including hit men and his inside connections in law enforcement—to track Juliette down and get rid of her, but is all what it seems?

Chapter One

Andre Diaz lurched upright, disoriented and unable to see through the thick smoke swirling in his bedroom. He sucked in a breath and instantly choked, even as his tired brain attempted to figure out what was happening.

"Andre! Get up!"

His older brother's voice cut through his growing fear and Andre threw off his covers and jumped out of bed, almost tripping.

"We have to move," Cole told him, his ever-calm voice laced with barely contained panic.

Andre stumbled through the dark room, each breath labored. Out in the hallway, light beckoned, but as he joined his brothers in the doorway, he realized it wasn't because someone had flicked a switch.

The house was on fire.

"Hold on to me," Cole insisted. "Marcos, grab Andre. Don't let go. Come on."

Andre clutched his older brother's shirt and he felt his younger brother's hand on his shoulder as the three of them hurried toward the stairwell. They ducked low to avoid the flames that seemed to be leaping all around them.

The walls were on fire. Andre looked up. The ceiling was on fire, too.

Finally, they reached the stairs and Cole picked up the pace. They were both coughing now, so whatever Cole yelled back at him, Andre couldn't understand.

His eyes were watering, too, and he couldn't see anything but flames lunging closer as he stumbled down the stairs, faster and faster, desperate for air. But every breath brought smoke deeper into his lungs.

Then, he could see it. The door was open. He could see outside.

But could he reach it? His lungs hurt, and his body was starting to shut down from lack of air. His eyes felt swollen and useless, and even though Cole was a step ahead of him, he knew it only because he still clutched his brother's shirt. All he could see was that open doorway ahead, the sun beginning to rise on the horizon.

But finally, he was stepping into the fresh air, falling onto the newly cut grass, coughing and coughing, feeling as if he'd never get oxygen into his aching throat.

Through his haze, he heard Cole screaming. Then he saw one word form on his brother's lips: "Marcos!"

Andre looked back and realized Marcos hadn't made it out behind him. The doorway he'd come through was now engulfed, flames reaching for the front porch.

Andre tried to get to his feet so he could race back to the house, but his knees kept buckling. Then Cole's arms were around him, holding him in place, even as Andre yelled for his younger brother. But no one else was coming through that flaming doorway, and suddenly sparks flew from the post on the front porch, and half of the roof collapsed.

Andre jerked awake in his bed, his heart thundering against his ribs. He was drenched in sweat, his breathing erratic, as though he was still inside that burning house.

"You got out," he reminded himself, throwing his covers aside and getting out of bed on unsteady feet. "We all got out."

The fire had happened eighteen years ago, when he'd been just fourteen. The first few years afterward, he'd woken up regularly, panicking until he remembered that his younger brother had escaped another way. He hadn't dreamed about that night in years.

But he knew what had brought it on: the call

he'd gotten last night at work. A family trapped inside their house. The father had set it on fire and was holding a gun on his wife and son, determined that they'd all die together. The firefighters couldn't go inside to save them without being shot.

The FBI had gotten the call from the local police, whose only sniper was out of commission. Andre's team had gone in, and he'd been the one to take the shot from the roof of the house across the street, through the second-story bedroom window.

He'd killed a man in front of his family, but it meant the firefighters had been able to enter the house. They'd gotten the wife and son out, alive and amazingly unharmed. Except for the nightmares they'd both surely have for years, too.

Beside his bed, a persistent buzzing caught his attention and he realized he'd been receiving texts. He swiped a hand over his forehead and grabbed the work cell phone he always kept close.

It was a triple-eight call from his boss at the FBI's elite Hostage Rescue Team, where he'd worked for the past four years as a sniper. Triple eight meant an emergency.

Of course, at HRT, they were already part of what the FBI called their Critical Incident Response Group. So no call was low priority. But triple eight was as high as it got.

It meant no time for even a two-minute shower, so he tossed aside the boxers he'd been wearing and traded them for cargos and a T-shirt, yanking up his flight suit over it. His FBI-issued rifle and the rest of the gear he carried on a mission were in a lockbox in the trunk of his sedan.

Andre double-timed it down the stairs of his little house and hopped in his car, still trying to shake off his dream, and hoping it wasn't an omen for what was to come today.

The information in the text was minimal, but it was enough to get his adrenaline going for a different reason. They were going to a hostage call at an office building not far from where he worked at Quantico. Multiple gunmen, multiple hostages.

At 7:00 a.m., the sun was just beginning to rise, and it instantly took him back to the dream he'd just left, those moments outside the house, frantic to get to Marcos. He slapped his siren on the roof, punched down on the gas and wove around a long line of cars. "Mind on the mission," he told himself.

He dialed his partner, Scott Delacorte, and soon Scott's gruff voice filled his car. "We don't know much. The gunmen are in a marketing company office up on the third floor. Employees there start early and leave early, to avoid some of the rush-hour traffic. So we could have a lot of hostages, but we're hoping none of the other companies in that building have started the day yet. Police are holding the scene."

"Any news on what the gunmen are after? Any communications? Do we know if they've fired shots?" Was this a hostage-taking situation or an active shooter?

"The call came in to 911 ten minutes ago from a secretary who managed to hide in the storage room. She told the operator there were multiple armed men—at least three—and at the time of the call, they hadn't started shooting. She thought they were searching for someone."

That might be good or bad. Good if the person they were after hadn't arrived yet; maybe the gunmen would leave, and HRT could nab them on the way out. Bad if the gunmen had a specific target they wanted to take out. Once they did, they might eliminate anyone else in their way.

Still, the setup was strange. A single gunman searching for a particular victim—maybe a spouse or stalking target—wasn't that unusual. But multiple gunmen, after one target? That was overkill. What single target at a small, independently owned marketing company would warrant that kind of firepower? It didn't quite fit.

"That's odd," was all Andre said aloud.

"Agreed. But the secretary's in the storage room. Who knows how well she's pegged the situation?" The screaming siren from Scott's end stopped. "I'm here. Gonna set up and get on the scope. Northwest corner, we've got woods, a nice trail that actually leads right out the back door of the office building and up a little hill. The whole thing is pretty hidden. I'm looking through my binoculars right now and I see a good sniper perch about a quarter mile up. How far out are you?"

"One minute."

"Make it faster," Scott said and cut the connection.

Andre pushed the gas pedal down to the floor, blaring his horn over the siren and whipping around the few drivers obnoxious enough not to get out of his way. Thirty seconds later, he was at the office complex.

He flashed his badge to the police officers stationed at the entrance to the complex, which was nestled in the woods. Thankfully it was off the beaten track enough that they shouldn't have to worry about the potential collateral of the pedestrians and gawkers they'd get if they were closer to the city.

The cops let him pass, and he flew into the parking lot, screeching to a stop next to his boss's big green SUV. He yanked his gear out of the trunk as his boss gave him the rundown.

"We don't know much more than what Scott already gave you," Froggy told him. The guy had been a navy SEAL before joining the FBI, and the nickname was a humorous nod to his past. "Go join Scott and get me some more intel."

"You got it." Andre slung his rifle over his back, slipped his gear bag over his shoulder and slid his Glock pistol out of the holster he'd put on while he drove. He popped his earbud in, and turned on the bone mic at his neck. It nestled against his voice box, so all he'd need to do was speak and his whole team could hear him. Then, he was on the move.

He ran around the corner of the office building, Glock ready in case one of the gunmen decided to try to rabbit out the back. Then he spotted the half-hidden trail Scott had mentioned and jogged onto it, increasing his pace even as the incline up the hill got more and more steep. Every minute counted for the hostages inside.

"I cleared you a spot," Scott said, not taking his eyes off the scope as Andre settled into the patch of dirt his partner indicated.

Andre dropped his gear beside him and set up his rifle, dialing in the specifics for wind and altitude that Scott read off to him. And then he was peering through his own rifle scope, into the third floor of the office building.

He scanned from left to right across the whole floor, taking in the situation. A gunman stood in the front room, a Bluetooth receiver in his ear and tattoos climbing out the top of his shirt. He clutched a semiautomatic pistol with both hands, but he kept checking the paper he held crumpled against the stock of his gun. On the floor around him were eight men and women in business clothes. Some held on to one another, two were in tears, and they were all avoiding the gunman's gaze as though he'd already warned them not to look at him. But no one appeared to be injured. Not yet.

Andre pulled back up to the gunman, dialing in a little closer, trying to see what was on the paper that was so interesting. He was speaking angrily, but Andre didn't think he was talking to the hostages.

"Phone's on," Scott said, seeming to read Andre's mind.

They'd been partners for two years now, and Scott had become practically a third brother to Andre. Half the time on missions, they didn't need words at all. "We know who he's talking to?"

"I think it's the second gunman."

Andre swung farther right and found the other

guy. He, too, had a cell phone, clipped to his waist, with an earphone in one ear. He held a semiautomatic, and he kept glaring down at a piece of paper as he wrenched open one door after the next, clearly searching for someone.

He pulled open another door and aimed his weapon at the woman cowering inside on the floor, surrounded by stacks of paper and printer cartridges. She yanked her hands up over her head, a phone dropping to the floor.

"Shit," Scott said as the gunman's grip shifted and Andre was able to zoom in closer and get a glimpse of what was on the paper he held.

"It's not her he's looking for," Andre said, keying his mic so the rest of the team could hear. "This guy's carrying a picture of a woman. Mid- to late-twenties, blondish-brown hair." A beautiful woman, with a sad smile. Not an easy face to miss. "She's not one of the hostages in the front room."

Andre widened his view again as the gunman waved the woman in the storage closet toward the other hostages. She scurried out of the room, then dropped down next to her coworkers, as the second guy continued to open doors, looking angrier and more frustrated with every empty room.

"I thought the secretary told us there were

at least three shooters," Andre said, continuing his search.

"She did, but I've only seen two. We've got operators in place right outside the front door. They're ready to storm the building if these guys start shooting, but ideally we identify the location of all the shooters first. If this goes bad, I've got the one with the hostages, okay? You take the other guy."

"Got it," Andre affirmed. But only Froggy could give the word to take any shots. If that happened, he'd have to shoot through the window and time it when the second gunman was in his line of sight, which could get dicey. The guy was heading into the back of the office now, where Andre didn't have an angle on him.

Scott swore and Andre asked what was wrong at the same time as Froggy.

"I found the last gunman."

"Where is he?" Andre asked, continuing his methodical search.

"He slipped out the back door. He's heading up the trail right now, straight for us. And the woman they were hunting for? She's with him, and he's got a gun pointed at her head."

Chapter Two

He'd found her. After all this time, she'd finally started to feel safe again, as if she didn't have to constantly look over her shoulder. But somehow, he'd found her and sent his goons after her.

These stupefied thoughts ran through Juliette Lawson's mind as she put one foot in front of the other. Her body had gone numb, but she could still feel the exact spot where the cold metal of a gun barrel pressed against her head.

The thug walking behind her had grabbed her just when she'd thought she was going to escape. She'd been in the bathroom when she'd heard screaming that morning. She'd peeked out in time to see three men enter, holding pictures of her. She'd never seen any of them before, but she knew why they'd come.

Initially, she'd darted back into the bathroom, hoping to hide, praying they wouldn't find her, that they'd just leave. But it soon became clear hiding wouldn't work, so she'd tried to slip down the back stairs. Just as she'd been reaching for the door to the exit, this one had come up behind her and put a gun to her head. He'd led her out the back door, out of sight of the police officers gathered in the distance and farther away from help.

She'd considered screaming, but fear had trapped it in her throat and then she'd realized if she did yell for help, he'd probably shoot.

Now, the gunman jabbed her with his weapon every few steps, pressuring her to move faster up the little dirt trail through the woods. But they were moving uphill at a steep angle, and she was wearing heels. If she picked up her pace any more, she was going to stumble. And the faster she walked, the less chance she had of figuring out a way to escape before he reached the next step of his plan.

Juliette knew the next step of his plan was to do one of two things: either get her somewhere secluded and kill her, or take her back to Dylan. It was like comparing a death sentence to life behind bars. She wasn't sure which was worse.

But she did know that if Dylan had hired him, this guy had training. Even if by some miracle, she managed to wrestle the gun away from him, he'd be able to take her down. If she ran, he'd probably shoot. And he wouldn't miss.

She tried to push aside all the regrets she felt, to focus on survival, but one regret kept surfacing. If only she'd never met Dylan Keane. Then maybe she'd still be back in Pennsylvania, still trying to sell the paintings she loved in galleries, instead of trying to be invisible as a graphic designer and spending her days buried in a cubicle.

Now there was a very good chance she wouldn't even be buried in a shallow grave. There was a good chance she was about to bleed out in the woods, and those cops who'd surrounded the office would eventually find her body. She prayed she'd be the only casualty, and the other gunmen wouldn't hurt her colleagues.

They had no idea who she really was, no idea what danger they were in just being near her. She'd never thought she'd been putting them in harm's way, because she'd never expected Dylan would send goons to her work. She'd always figured that if he tracked her down, he'd simply grab her out of her apartment one day and drag her back. Force her to live in that house again, like a prisoner. Or just kill her right there and leave her dead in her apartment until one of her neighbors noticed the smell.

Stop it, Juliette told herself. Morose thoughts weren't going to get her out of this. She needed a plan. And even though running was pointless, it was probably her best chance.

Up ahead, the trail curved. That was the spot. She'd pretend to stumble, ditch the heels. She'd be able to run faster barefoot.

Her heart started pounding so hard she could hear the blood pumping in her ears. It seemed to block out the other noises off in the distance— the birds chirping, the FBI agent in the parking lot yelling over a loudspeaker at the gunmen, even the big, furious guy behind her insisting she pick up her pace.

The curve got closer and closer, until she knew it was time. Her heart felt out of control as she let out a squeak and pretended to trip on a protruding branch, going down on her knees and sliding out of her heels as though they'd come off in the fall. The guy's hand closed around her arm, but the gun came down. It was no longer pointed at her head.

This was her chance.

She readied herself to shove upward, to knock him down and run as fast as she could, zigging and zagging the way Dylan had taught her, back before he realized he might not want her to escape a bullet. But she never had the chance to try.

A figure flew out of a tree, crashing past her and onto her attacker in a tangled blur of arms and legs and guns.

Juliette yelped and scurried free. The new

man was armed too, a Glock strapped to his hip, and a whole slew of other equipment attached to his body that suggested he was in the military. He was all motion, just smooth brown skin and bulging muscles and full of confidence as he drew back a fist and sent it crashing into the gunman's jaw.

The gunman took the hit with a growl and tried to flip the new guy, but Juliette didn't wait around to see who'd come out on top or how long the fight would last. She caught a glimpse of intense, dark brown eyes on her rescuer and decided he was some kind of Special Operations soldier. She had no idea what he was doing in the woods, but she said a silent *thank you* and stumbled to her feet, darting off the trail.

She was pretty sure the soldier was going to prevail in the fight happening behind her, but even if he wasn't with the law enforcement surrounding the office complex, he'd surely turn her over to them.

And then there was no question what would happen next: she'd be headed straight back to Dylan, straight back to the life she thought she'd finally escaped.

"WHAT DO YOU think you're doing?"

A strong hand closed around her arm, bringing Juliette to a stop. Her bare feet almost slid out from underneath her on the trail, which was slippery from the leaves that had begun falling off the trees a week ago. Before she could go down, her rescuer dropped his hand from her arm to her waist, catching her.

"It's over," he said, his voice reassuring. His fingers pressed into the top of her hip, keeping her from making another run for it, away from everyone. "The guy's in handcuffs. You're safe."

Juliette stared up at him. He probably had four inches on her height of five foot six, just enough so she had to tip her head back to look him in the eyes. They were deep brown, almost hypnotizing the way they were locked onto hers as though he didn't see anything else in the world right now.

She knew it was only because he was trying to convince her everything was going to be okay, but that didn't stop a shiver of awareness from working its way up from her toes.

Thank goodness he misunderstood the reason. He told her, "I'm Andre Diaz, with the FBI. I promise you, you're safe with me, okay? And we're going to get your colleagues out of there. But right now, I need you to come with me."

Instead of letting go of her waist, he led her back down the trail toward the parking lot, guiding her like she was in shock. Which maybe she was, because she couldn't believe any of this was happening.

She'd been on the run for three years. She'd managed to hide, to somehow stay one step ahead of Dylan all that time. And now it was over.

Those first few months, heck, that entire first year, she'd jumped at every noise and slept with the lights on most nights. But lately, she'd found herself relaxing. She couldn't remember the last time she'd looked over her shoulder or run to her car clutching her mace in one hand, certain one of Dylan's lackeys was on her trail.

She'd let her guard down, created a new life for herself. It hadn't been a full life, but it had been *hers*. And now it was over.

Glancing at Andre as he helped her down the trail, carefully avoiding any sharp sticks or rocks on the trail because of her bare feet, tears blurred her vision. Not out of fear, but because someone cared enough to bother helping her. She blinked them away.

Now wasn't the time to get emotional because some guy was doing his job, because apparently some members of law enforcement really were on the side of the victims. And now *really* wasn't the time to fixate on the feel of his strong hand grasping the top of her hip as he led her to all those blinking red and blue lights in front of her office building. But she couldn't help but be hyperaware of the pure masculine scent of him beside her, the ridiculously hard bicep pressing into her back.

She dragged her feet as they hit the concrete, glancing up at the third floor where all her colleagues were, terrified because of her. And she realized Andre had carefully led her to a vehicle on a path that kept her completely out of view of the windows up on the third floor.

"Hop in here," he told her, holding open the back of an SUV with tinted windows. When she hesitated, he added, "It's my boss's vehicle. You'll be okay. It's surrounded by my team, and there's no way anyone's getting past them. When this is over, we'll get you home safely."

She hesitated once more, because she could never go home again. Not to any of the places she'd ever called home over the years.

Then, the *tat, tat, tat* of a semiautomatic boomed, followed by two more shots in quick succession, and someone let out a piercing scream.

Juliette spun toward the sound, dreading what she was going to see—who had gotten hurt because of her. But she never found out, because Andre shoved her into the SUV and dove on top of her.

The weight of him flattened all the air from

her lungs, and the awareness she'd felt earlier when he'd simply had his hand on her waist multiplied, making her skin seem to buzz wherever it touched his. Even though he was simply protecting her, she was suddenly keenly aware of how long it had been since someone had held her.

She tried not to squirm and prayed she wasn't flushed deep red as he spoke into some kind of communications device she realized went from his ear to a microphone at his neck. Then just as quickly, he was helping her up.

She felt dazed, still trying to catch her breath as he told her, "It's over. All of your colleagues are okay."

"What?" The word came out breathy and filled with disbelief. How could it possibly be over that fast? And how could everyone be unharmed?

He gave her a grin that made a dimple pop on one side and said, "We're good at what we do."

She stared back at him, taking in all the details she hadn't noticed before: his cleanly shaved head, the cleft in his chin, the complete focus in his eyes. Beneath that, genuine warmth, as if he really cared what happened to her and it wasn't just his job to keep her safe for the next few minutes.

Don't fall for him, she chanted in her head.

She'd just met him. She knew nothing about him, other than that he was willing to put his life on the line for others.

She'd fallen for Dylan that way: instantly. A sudden, ridiculous attraction that she'd mistakenly thought was love. She'd fallen for all the things she thought she'd seen in him that had turned out not to be true. And she was seeing all those qualities in Andre's eyes right now: the goodness, the honesty, the protectiveness. Except she suspected with Andre, they were actually real.

His gaze seemed to bore into her and then she saw something else: a reciprocal glint of attraction. It made her want to lean closer and tell him the truth about what had happened today. To go through the process she knew they'd want: hours of questioning at some police station or maybe an FBI office, to learn why hired gunmen were after her. To trust that maybe this time someone would believe her story. That maybe this time things could really change. But she couldn't take the chance.

He smiled at her and gave her a hand out of the vehicle.

One of the other agents, dressed as if he was going to war, slapped him on the back and said, "Why don't you give her a ride back to Quantico? The locals are asking us to take the lead, since these gunmen might be professionals. We're going to need a debrief."

She could tell from Andre's dimpled smile that when the questioning was over, he was going to ask her out. In another life, she would have said *yes*.

Too bad she'd never see him again after today.

"AREN'T YOU GOING to stick around and see if you can drive this woman home?" Scott teased, just as Andre thought he'd made a clean getaway.

Andre spun around in the Quantico parking lot, where they'd driven after the situation was contained. The gunman who'd fired in that office had been shot by one of HRT's operators, but the other two had been brought in wearing handcuffs. They had both gone silent as soon as they were arrested, demanding lawyers, but the FBI had been able to ID them quickly anyway, because they had criminal records. Strangely, the woman Scott was talking about had gone just as silent as the gunmen. She claimed she didn't know why they were after her, when clearly she did.

"Which woman?" Andre parried, even though he knew Scott wasn't about to let him off the hook that easily.

"Juliette. Or was it Mya?"

That was the other problem. The woman he'd

rescued on that hill had identified herself as Juliette Lawson. So had her colleagues. But the name scrawled next to her picture that the gunmen had all been carrying was *Mya*.

When they'd mentioned it to Juliette, she'd gone pale and made a beeline for the women's bathroom, where she'd been for the past hour, either sick or just hiding out.

The fact was, Andre *had* planned to ask her out. From the second their eyes had met inside his boss's SUV, he'd known he was in trouble. Sure, she was gorgeous, with those wide hazel eyes framed with insanely dark lashes, and all that long, golden-tinted brown hair that had come loose from her messy bun when he'd tackled her. The soft, womanly curves that had cushioned his fall were pretty tempting, too. But what had really done him in was the way she'd stared back at him, the look in her eyes equal parts vulnerable and strong.

He'd driven her back to Quantico, making small talk on the ride, trying to get to know her a little better. She'd seemed shy, shell-shocked, but definitely interested. He'd intended to wait around until the regular agents had finished questioning her, then ask if he could make a detour to dinner on the way back to her car. But that was when he'd thought she was a simple victim.

He should have known from the beginning there was more to it, because the crime itself was so strange. Why send three heavily armed men after one small woman in a third-floor office building?

In fact, why do it in such a high-profile way at all? Why not have one man grab her on the way to her car before she made it into the office?

She was involved in something. The fact was, she was probably guilty of something. And while a woman with a little mystery had always been a draw for him, a woman who would break the law he worked to uphold was of no interest.

Andre shrugged at his partner, who'd been his friend too long not to see exactly what Andre wasn't saying. "I'm not sure I need that kind of drama."

"There's always Nadia," Scott said.

Nadia Petrova was a fellow agent, who worked as a weapons training specialist at the FBI Academy, which was located at Quantico with HRT. She'd made no secret of her interest in Andre, and it was getting more and more difficult to sidestep her hints without hurting her feelings.

"I think I want to be the one in the relationship with the bigger guns," Andre joked. The truth was, Nadia was nice enough, but there just wasn't any spark.

Scott snorted and slapped him on the arm.

"All right. Well, after these last couple of calls back-to-back, I'm heading home. Froggy says you can do the same if you want. The other team is up now."

The HRT teams swapped off, so one was always on call if any emergencies came in from across the country while the other teams trained. After the week they'd had, with seemingly one crisis after the next, Andre was ready for some low-key exercises. Like rappelling out of helicopters and practicing with his MP5 for mock hostage situations inside one of the old 747-airplane hulls they kept on hand.

"See you tomorrow," Andre said, digging around in his duffel for wherever he'd stuck his keys as Scott hopped in his SUV and sped away, leaving Andre alone in a lot full of cars but empty of people.

When he'd pulled into the lot a few hours ago, there had been nowhere left to park except at the very back, so he meandered that way now, still digging for his keys. It wasn't until he was a few feet away from his sedan that his agent instincts went on high alert, warning him someone was close. Too close.

He lifted his hands into a defensive position even as his brain reminded him he was in a heavily guarded Marine base and FBI training area. Then he let out a breath and dropped his hands to his sides as he spotted Juliette—or Mya—coming around from the front of his car.

"What are you doing here?" Had she been waiting for him, crouched between the grill of his car and the big tree he'd parked underneath for a little shade? He frowned. Had she been hiding?

"Get in the car," she said, her voice wobbly.

A smile threatened. "That's what I was planning," he said, starting to rethink his plan to ask her out to dinner. Except… "Shouldn't you still be inside, talking to the case agents?"

The hand that had been wedged between her side and his car came out, pointing a Glock pistol at him. "Get in." This time, her tone was apologetic.

He stared, dumbfounded. "Where'd you get that?" She certainly hadn't come into Quantico with a weapon. Had she taken it off someone inside? If so, that meant she was a much bigger threat than she seemed.

"I'm sorry," she said, and she actually looked it, with her big, teary eyes and her full, trembling lips. "But we need to go. I have to get out of here, which means you're going to drive me off the base."

He leaned against his car, eyeing the distance between them, gauging whether he could disarm her without the gun going off. "Why don't you tell me what this is about? Let me help you." He kept his voice calm. It was the same tone he'd used last night with the traumatized kid who'd come out of that fire clutching his mother, after watching a bullet come through the window and take out his father.

"No. Please." Desperation entered her tone as she shifted her awkward, double-handed hold on the gun. "Just get in, okay, and I promise I'll let you go as soon as you drop me off where I tell you."

She wasn't used to holding a weapon, Andre could tell. "You're going to have a hard time firing that gun with the safety on."

When she glanced down, he took one slow step forward, almost close enough to disarm her without a chance of her taking a shot. Just one more step and he could do it.

But then her eyes locked on his as she leveled the weapon at his center mass, something hard and determined in her gaze. "There's no external safety on a Glock," she replied, all the nerves gone from her voice. "Now get in. We're going for a ride."

Chapter Three

She'd just taken a federal agent hostage.

And not just any federal agent. No, she'd picked some kind of super-agent, a man who could take down an armed criminal with his bare hands. When he'd flattened her against the floor of his boss's SUV a few hours ago, she'd discovered he probably had a negative percentage of body fat. He was all hard, solid muscle.

She should be afraid of what he could do with that muscle, especially after her actions tonight, but for some reason, he made her feel safe.

Andre's hands were tense on the wheel as he drove silently away from Quantico. He hadn't said a word since they'd gotten in the car and driven past the guard and out of the gated complex. But she knew that wouldn't last much longer.

What she didn't know was what she was going to say to him.

It didn't matter that she'd emptied the gun of its bullets back in the FBI office after she'd slipped it out of an agent's holster. There was still no excuse for what she'd just done. Not even if it might well save her life.

The armed standoff at her office building had surely made the news by now. Dylan would know his goons had failed. What's more, he'd know where to find her himself. Heck, if he wanted to, he could probably get into Quantico and drive her away without anyone making a word of protest. Why would they question a fellow law enforcement officer?

"You planning to tell me what this is all about?"

Andre's question was quiet, almost a whisper, but it still made Juliette jump in her seat as his voice brought her out of her reverie.

"And would you mind aiming that gun somewhere else? I'd prefer it if you didn't shoot me accidentally."

"I'm not going to shoot you at all," Juliette blurted, then silently cursed herself.

But her words didn't seem to surprise him. He just repeated his request, and she set the gun on her lap, close enough that she could grab it, but not pointed at him anymore.

"Where are we going?" he asked when she didn't say any more.

She'd directed him to drive out of Quantico but hadn't given him a location beyond that. The truth was, she had no idea where she was going. Back to her office—where her car was—was a bad idea, because police were surely still there. And by now, Dylan would have both her work and home address.

Her apartment was off limits. All the things she'd worked hard to build for herself here, she'd have to leave behind. But that was a small price to pay for her life.

She'd planned to have Andre drop her off somewhere she could hitchhike out of town. But the exact logistics of getting out of town before the FBI found and arrested her? She hadn't quite figured those out.

He must have sensed her hesitation, because he suggested, "How about I drive you to my place?"

"What?" She gaped at him. Was this some kind of trick?

"You obviously have nowhere to go," Andre said, his voice tired. "And I think you need help. Let *me* help you."

"I just repaid you for saving my life by taking you hostage!" Juliette flushed as she said it, both at the absurdity of what she'd done and at how ridiculous she was to argue with him if he was really willing to hear her out.

"You also told me you weren't going to shoot me," Andre replied, still sounding calm and in control, even though she was the one holding the gun.

A gun that as far as he knew was loaded with bullets. And one she'd proven she knew how to use when she'd told him the Glock didn't have an external safety.

This had to be a trick. But what choice did she really have? She was tired of running. She wanted her life back. She wanted a *real* life back. Maybe if she let herself trust him, just for now, Andre could help her get that.

"Okay," Juliette agreed, amazed the words were coming out of her mouth even as she said them. "Let's go to your place."

THIS WAS A *bad idea.*

The words echoing in Andre's head sounded like his older brother, Cole. And even though it was his experience that Cole was almost always right, Andre pushed them aside and held open the door to his house for Juliette.

He watched her glance around the living room curiously, taking in the oversize couch, the comfortable chairs bracketing it, the coffee table stacked with books and coasters. He knew it appeared lived in, the kind of place often over-flowing with friends and family. She lingered on

the photos lining the table behind his couch—
he and his brothers, he and Scott on an overseas
mission, his HRT team after a joint training with
some navy SEALs. His families.

"You have a nice home," she said softly. "It's
cozy."

There was something wistful in her tone, as
though she didn't have memories scattered all
around her own place. But for some reason, he
had a hard time imagining her *not* surrounded
by people. Instead of asking about it, he said
simply, "Thanks. Make yourself comfortable."

Right now, she seemed as far from comfortable as possible. She'd left her heels somewhere
in the woods, so she'd been barefoot ever since,
the hem of her slacks collecting dust. She had
one hand crammed into the pocket of her cardigan, the outline of the Glock clearly visible.
Her hair was a mess, with a few bobby pins val-
iantly trying to hold up what had started out as
a bun, and leaves woven through strands that
shimmered under the light. Her pale skin had
been flushed from the moment she'd pointed
the gun at him.

Maybe if he could get her to relax, he could
get a real story out of her. And then he could decide on his next move.

When she just shifted her weight from one
foot to the other right inside his door, he closed

it behind her and flopped onto his couch across the room, careful not to let the hem of his T-shirt come up. So far, she hadn't thought to ask, and he didn't want to give her reason to suspect he was armed. He might be willing to bring her to his house, but there was no way he was handing over his gun.

He was giving her a lot more benefit of the doubt than he normally would. Maybe it was the attraction he'd felt for her the second he'd seen her. More likely it was the vulnerability he kept seeing. He was a sucker for a damsel in distress.

The only problem was, there was a good chance Juliette was involved in something she shouldn't be. At the very least, she'd taken a weapon off someone, and he couldn't forget that meant she was more dangerous than she appeared.

Still, he needed her to trust him if they were going to get anywhere. He'd figure out the rest of it from there.

"Have you lived in Virginia very long?" he asked, his tone easy and casual.

She eyed him as though wondering what his angle was, but he just waited patiently, hoping to ease her into conversation.

Finally, she took some hesitant steps forward and settled gingerly on the edge of one of his chairs, far away from him. "A little while."

"I've been here for four years, ever since I got accepted into HRT." When she looked perplexed, he clarified, "The FBI's Hostage Rescue Team. The tryouts were brutal, and when they put me in a sniper role, I had to go through extra training with the marines."

She leaned back into her chair a bit, her expression intrigued, so he kept going.

"The guy you met today, the one who came down that trail we were on? That was my partner, Scott. We've worked together for two years. He's practically my third brother now." He paused, hoping she'd engage, that he could connect with her and get a real story about what had happened today.

"You have two brothers?" Her gaze went back to the photos, probably searching for someone with any kind of genetic similarity.

"You'll never pick them out," he said with a smile. "They're my foster brothers. We look nothing alike. But we're closer than blood." Even after the fire that had destroyed their house, that had very nearly taken Marcos's life, and had split them apart into separate foster homes, they'd managed to remain family.

"That's nice," she replied, and there it was again, that wistful tone.

"You're not close to your family?"

"No. I grew up in boarding schools." She said it without anger, just a hint of sadness.

Andre cringed. He only had a vague memory of his biological family, before they'd died in a boating accident when he was five. But that vague memory was tied up in his mother's arms, holding him close; in his father's voice, reading him stories. And he had five years of a true, brotherly bond with Cole and Marcos in his second foster home. But before and after that? He knew what it was like to feel all alone, to do his best to go unnoticed because that was the safest way.

He silently cursed. He was already sucked into those wide hazel eyes. He didn't need any more reasons to feel tied to her, to protect her at all costs, even if she really belonged in jail. His gaze shifted to the bulge in her sweater where she'd stuffed the gun.

"Do you want to tell me what really happened today, Juliette? Who were those men after you?"

"I don't know."

He must have looked skeptical, because she immediately insisted, "I don't know them. But I know who hired them. They had criminal records, right? Probably in Pennsylvania?"

He leaned forward. "How did you know that?"

Her face pinched. "Because my ex-husband hired them to kidnap me."

"Your ex-husband?" Andre tried to keep the surprise off his face. He didn't know why he'd expected her never to have been married. It shouldn't matter one way or another, but he found himself disappointed. "Why would he want to kidnap you?"

She gave him a sad smile. "Let's just say that the divorce wasn't amicable. Hell, I don't even know if it's official. I filed, and then I ran. But in order for it to be approved, he has to agree to no-fault. I didn't want to go through a court date, so I didn't dare file a fault complaint."

She fidgeted on the chair, avoiding his gaze, and he knew there was more to the story. Probably a lot more.

Anger heated him, and memories flashed through his mind, images he didn't want to dwell on, from his first foster home. "Did he hurt you?"

"No." She shook her head, but still didn't meet his eyes. "But I saw something I shouldn't have seen, and he knew it. I tried to tell him I'd keep his secret, just to get him to let me go, but he wanted me close. So when I finally accepted that I was in danger, that I had to go, I just filed and ran."

"Why were you in danger?" Andre forced himself not to lean forward, not to show the aggression he was feeling toward her ex. "Why didn't you just go to the police for help? Get a restraining order against him?"

She let out a heavy breath. "I couldn't do that. He was…"

"He was what?" Andre pressed when she went silent for too long. Then his phone rang, and he saw her tense even before he checked the readout. Scott was calling.

He considered letting it go to voice mail, but if someone had spotted Juliette holding a gun on him, he didn't want his teammates swarming his house in a misguided rescue attempt. "I need to answer this," he told her. "But you're safe here, okay?"

He didn't let her argue, just picked up his cell. "Scott. What's going on?"

"You didn't see that woman—Juliette or Mya or whatever her name is—sneak out, did you?"

"Why?" Andre asked, instead of answering, because he hated lying to family.

"She left before they could question her," Scott said. "You're not going to believe this, but she actually managed to get a weapon off of Nadia in the restroom."

"Is Nadia hurt?" If Juliette had disarmed a weapons training agent who could bring fellow agents to tears using her chokehold techniques on the training mats, then Juliette was much more dangerous than he'd suspected.

"Nah, Nadia's fine. Mostly embarrassed. Apparently this woman has sticky fingers."

So, Juliette was a pickpocket. Somehow, that didn't fit. But then nothing about Juliette had fit so far. Still, taking a wallet from an unsuspecting mark on the street was a lot different from getting an agent's weapon out of its holster.

"Anyway, there's a lot more to this story," Scott continued. "And the FBI thinks the woman's in danger."

Andre's gaze sought Juliette's. She stared back at him, her eyes wide.

"What did they get from the gunmen? Are they talking yet?"

"Yeah. I spoke to Froggy. Turns out they took an initial payment for grabbing this woman, and they were expecting more when the job was finished."

"Who paid them?" Was Juliette right? Was it her ex?

"These idiots are claiming they don't know. Which is either true, or they'd worked out their stories together beforehand. They say they were approached anonymously, that it was supposed to be easy money. Grab her, do the job, then get the other half of the money when the deal was complete."

"And they didn't think it was some kind of setup? Or just take the first payment and run?"

Scott sighed. "They both seem to think a cop hired them."

"A cop?" Andre scoffed. "They think a cop hired a pack of ex-cons to kidnap a marketing employee at gunpoint out of her workplace?" He watched Juliette go pale and frowned. "That makes no sense at all. What kind of cop would send these guys in on such a flawed plan?"

"Well, it wasn't the original plan," Scott said. "Right now, because the third guy fired in that office building on FBI agents and they're all going to face some serious sentences, the two we've got in custody are tripping over each other trying to make deals. The case agents have them separated, but they're getting the same story."

"What are they saying?"

"The hostage grab out of the office building was the *criminals'* plan. They wanted it to hit the news, so their anonymous employer would see it. They were planning to grab her and demand a higher payout for her delivery."

"Okay," Andre said slowly. "That does make more sense. So, the original plan was to grab her more quietly, then make the trade in some deserted location? Juliette for the money?"

"I wish that was the case," Scott answered. "But the plan wasn't to grab her at all. And apparently the second guy—the one you tackled on the path—was trying to double-cross the other two and get all the money for himself, so there's no love lost there."

"So what *was* the plan?" Andre demanded, a bad feeling settling in his stomach as Juliette's words came back to him, her fear of taking her ex-husband to court. And suddenly he knew. Her ex-husband was a cop. Her ex-husband was *the* cop, the one who'd hired three dangerous ex-cons to grab Juliette.

He watched her hands clutch the arms of his chair until her knuckles were bone white. And he could tell she knew the answer to his question without even hearing Scott's reply.

"They were supposed to kill her, Andre. They were told to snatch her quietly, drive her somewhere secluded, kill her and bury the body."

"This was never supposed to go public," Andre said, not taking his eyes off of Juliette.

"No. This woman was supposed to just disappear forever."

Chapter Four

"I need the truth."

Juliette bristled. "I'm not lying to you."

"How'd you learn to snatch a weapon off a law enforcement official?" Andre demanded, resting his forearms on his thighs, making all the muscles in his arms tense and reminding her that he wasn't just strong.

He was also fast.

Juliette scooted to the edge of the chair, in case she needed to make a quick getaway. What had she been thinking, coming here? She glanced at the doorway, gauging the distance.

"Too far," Andre said.

"What?" Panic hitched her voice.

"You're thinking of making a run for it. I'm telling you that you won't make it."

She put her hand on the gun in her pocket, her heart thudding frantically. What if Andre had given his partner some kind of code word in their conversation? Something to let him know to send the cavalry? If they believed Dylan instead of her...

"I'm trying to help you here," Andre said, his soft voice laced with frustration. "We just determined these thugs were supposed to kill you."

She cringed, even though it wasn't news at all. She'd known the second she'd spotted them holding her picture that Dylan had decided to kill her. That it didn't matter those years they'd spent dating, falling in love. That it didn't matter they'd pledged their lives to each other.

"Do you really think it's your best move to run, alone?" Andre interrupted her angry thoughts. "We can protect you."

"Against someone else in law enforcement?" Juliette snapped. "I've tried before. Who is anyone going to believe, me or another cop?"

He stared directly into her eyes, intense and sincere. "*I* believe you."

She stamped down the hope she felt at his words and tried to be logical. "Why?"

"You work in this job long enough and you learn. All the training, all the practice, can only take you so far. At a certain point, you just have to go with your gut. And my gut is telling me you're innocent." His gaze went to the gun and then back to her face. "Relatively innocent."

A smile twitched her lips with a sudden, ridiculous urge to laugh at the predicament she'd gotten herself into. She'd never so much as gotten a parking ticket her whole life, and in one day she'd stolen a gun off one federal agent and taken another one hostage. The truth was, they had more on her than anyone had ever gotten on her ex-husband. The smile faded.

"Just level with me, Juliette," Andre said, his deep brown eyes imploring, almost hypnotizing in their intensity.

A shiver worked its way up her body that had nothing to do with fear and she suppressed it. Letting her attraction for this man lull her into trusting him was a bad idea. No matter whether or not he believed her story, he was still a federal agent. It was still his job to make sure she answered questions about what had happened today, and after her actions over the past hour, the FBI would probably expect her to do it in handcuffs.

Besides, she'd done the whole falling hard for a man with a badge thing before, and it hadn't worked out too well for her then. She doubted things would go better a second time.

"I told you the truth. Okay, so I said he wanted to kidnap me, and I guess that was wishful thinking. I suppose I knew it. Dylan wants me dead. I've been running for years, and now he's found me. And you can believe if he—or one of his hired goons—catches up to me again, he won't make the same mistake."

"You saw something you shouldn't have seen," he repeated her words from earlier. "What was it?"

Juliette heaved out a sigh. "Not enough."

"What does that mean?"

She'd come this far. The man had brought her to his house. He was the first person in years she'd dared to tell even this much. Might as well go for broke.

"My ex was a cop—*is* a cop. I actually met him when he pulled me over for a broken taillight. He let me go with a warning, but when I ran into him a few weeks later at a club, he asked me out."

At the time, she'd thought it was some kind of fate, telling her to give Dylan a chance. Later, she'd learned that he'd run her plates, gotten her name and pulled her up on social media. Someone had tagged her at that club, and he'd gone there, specifically intending to bump into her. When he'd finally told her the truth on their honeymoon, she'd been flattered. Now she wondered if it had been a warning sign she'd been too infatuated to see.

"What's his name?" Andre asked tightly.

"Dylan. Dylan Keane."

"From Pennsylvania?"

"That's right. But if you're planning to dig up his file, don't bother. He's got a perfect record at the department. He actually got a commendation from the mayor right after we were married. No one will ever believe he's dirty."

"That's what this is about?" Andre pressed. "That's what you saw? Something to do with his work?"

"Yeah. Have you ever heard of Kent Manning?"

Andre's eyes narrowed and his head tilted back, as though he was trying to remember where he'd heard the name.

"The businessman who was killed," she prompted.

"That's right. He was a multimillionaire, if I'm remembering correctly. They found him tossed in the lake in some small town in…"

She could tell the instant he realized. "Right. A small town in Pennsylvania. *My* small town in Pennsylvania."

"But they caught the guy who killed him. He's serving a life sentence, isn't he?"

"He is. Chester Loews was Manning's direct competitor. With Manning out of the picture, Loews's company was poised to become the biggest logging supplier in the state."

"All right. That's a logical motive for murder. What does all of this have to do with your husband?"

"*Ex*-husband."

"Sorry." Andre gave her a half smile that made a dimple pop in his left cheek. "Believe me, I didn't forget that part."

Juliette swallowed, her mouth dry, and wondered what the heck that meant. Was it because he was interested in her?

Get it together, she reminded herself. "Anyway," she continued, hoping she wasn't flushed beet red, "what I overheard was my husband meeting with Boyd Harkin. He was Manning's second-in-command, and when Manning was murdered, Harkin took over the company. He was originally a suspect, too, but the evidence against Loews was so overwhelming, it was a slam dunk. Case closed."

"But you think Harkin actually killed Manning?" Andre guessed. "You think Loews was framed?"

"I think they were working together and only Loews got caught."

Andre frowned. "If that's the case, then why wouldn't Loews turn on Harkin? Share the prison sentence?"

"I don't know."

"Okay." He was clearly trying hard to be

patient. "Why do you think they were working together?"

"My ex-husband and his partner were working the Manning murder case, and I saw Harkin hand my ex-husband a bag." She'd come home early, unexpected, from her studio because she'd been sick. Harkin had been standing in her kitchen, a big hulk of a man who looked unnatural in a business suit. He'd handed over a brown paper bag, as though he was playing a part in a movie. "Dylan told Harkin he'd keep him out of it, but there was nothing he could do for Loews now."

"Those were his exact words?" Andre asked.

"Yeah. I thought Dylan was getting the bag to make sure any evidence against Harkin found during the murder investigation would disappear."

From the way Andre was nodding, he agreed. "And you think that bag contained a payoff?"

"I know it did. I found it later, stashed up in our closet. Dylan thought I didn't know he hid things there, but I'd seen him do it before."

"You'd seen him take money before?"

"No." She gave a sad smile, because not all of her memories of Dylan were bad. She'd loved him once, enough to marry him. "Presents he'd bought me."

Andre nodded, understanding on his face.

"So, what made you run? Did Dylan know you'd spotted him and Harkin?"

"No. They were so busy talking, they never heard me come in."

"Did he notice the money was moved? What?"

"No. Worse."

"You confronted him."

It wasn't a question, but Juliette answered anyway. "Yes. At first I was sure Dylan would turn him in, but every few days I'd check, and the money was still there. So finally I asked him. I thought for sure he'd tell me there was an undercover operation happening, that they were going to arrest Harkin any day now."

The memory burst forward in her mind, the moment she'd replayed so many times in the past three years. At first, she'd wished she could take it back, that she'd never seen Dylan accept the money, that she could just stay ignorant. Then, she'd wished to take back different moments, like the instant she'd said *yes* to his marriage proposal, practically before he could get the question out. Even the more hesitant *yes* when he'd first asked her out.

"He came home late because he'd been working a big case, but all excited about some cabin one of his buddies was going to lend him for the weekend. He wanted us to go away, just the two of us. Then I told him what I'd seen, and I knew the second I did it that our marriage was over."

Sadness and pity and some other emotion she couldn't quite pinpoint flashed across Andre's face, and she got back to what mattered now. "He told me I needed to forget I'd ever heard that conversation."

A tremor went through her, recalling the fury in Dylan's voice, the hard glint she'd never seen before in his eyes. "He said if I ever told anyone, I was signing my own death warrant."

ANDRE FOUGHT HARD to keep his expression neutral, not to let Juliette see how badly he wanted to smash her ex's face in with his fist right now. He was pretty sure he was failing miserably.

She gave him a shaky smile. "This is why I was trying to run. I can't have my name connected to any kind of investigation or he'll find me."

"You do know there's not some kind of law enforcement bulletin that goes out with everyone's active cases, right?" Andre joked.

"Yeah, well, when the hostage situation hits the news—if it hasn't already—he'll know I'm here. The first thing he'll do is contact the FBI."

"I doubt it. That'd be pretty suspicious."

She snorted. It should have been ugly, but somehow it was cute. "Trust me, he'll come up with a story everyone will believe. He's done it before."

"What do you mean?" Andre asked, remembering her comment that she'd tried to get help in the past, and no one had believed her. "You tried to report him, didn't you?"

"Yeah." She sighed and sank back into the chair, her head dropping back and her hands going limp at her sides.

It would be easy to jump up and snatch the gun off her lap now, but he didn't. He just waited for her to start talking.

"Stupidly, I went to my local department, where he worked."

"That's not stupid. It's logical," Andre said, even though she probably should have gone to the FBI.

"Maybe it would have made a difference if I'd done it that night, instead of waiting to see if I'd misunderstood. But by the time I finally got the courage to turn him in, he'd already set the groundwork. They were expecting me. He'd told the chief that I'd..." She flushed, her voice getting quieter as she finished, "That I'd had a miscarriage and was suffering from severe depression."

"Did you?" Andre asked quietly, not even realizing that he'd reached out to take her hand until she lifted her head and looked at it, perplexed.

But she didn't pull hers away. She just shook her head and continued, "No. But he said the doctor had put me on medication and I was having delusions that everyone was out to get me."

"And they bought it?" Andre asked with disbelief. "Even when you told them specifics about the money?"

"I never got that far. I tried to talk about Dylan meeting with Harkin, but they just patted me on my head and sent me home. The chief *literally* patted my head, as if I was a child. And when I got home that night…" She trailed off, as a shiver visibly went through her. "Anyway, that was when I knew I had to run. And I've been running ever since."

"Three years," Andre said, doing the math from the time he remembered seeing Manning's death in the news.

"Yeah. Twice before, he's caught up to me, but I managed to keep running, start over yet again. I thought this time I'd finally gotten away. I should have known better. I'm never going to be free of this."

"Everything is different now," Andre promised her.

"How?"

"This time, you've got help." Andre squeezed her hand. "We're going to nail him to the wall for this."

He could see hope spark in her eyes, but just as quickly, she seemed to push it down. She carefully pulled her hand free and twisted it nervously in her lap. "How? All we have is the word of two criminals who don't even know who hired them. And me. A woman using an assumed name who's probably got a warrant out for her arrest now, too."

Andre's mind warred with what to ask next— how she'd managed to get that gun off Nadia in order to earn that possible warrant or what her real name was. He should ask about the gun, since knowing her ex's name meant he could track hers down. But somehow, the question that came out of his mouth was, "What's your real name? It's Mya, isn't it?"

Her nose crinkled. "Technically, yeah. But Juliette's my middle name. I've gone by Juliette most of my life."

"Kind of a strange choice for a fake name, then," Andre commented.

"Yeah, probably, but I'm sure Dylan expected me to use Mya and a different last name." He must have looked confused, because she added, "He called me Mya. He was the only one who did when we met, and we were only married for a year, but over the time we knew each other, my social circle just kept shrinking, and somehow

I ended up in his. So by the end, no one called me Juliette anymore."

"Controlling," Andre muttered.

"It's not what you think. He wasn't cruel or abusive or anything, just…" She seemed to search for the right word, finally settling on *manipulative*.

Andre thought about arguing, because her relationship with her husband sure sounded abusive—maybe not physically but definitely psychologically. But the truth was, no matter the attraction he'd felt from the second he'd met her or how he wanted to help her now, her relationship with her ex wasn't any of his business. So instead he just said, "You wanted to reclaim the name for yourself."

"Exactly. I wasn't Mya Moreau anymore or Mya Keane. I was Juliette Lawson. Lawson was my grandma's maiden name." She fidgeted. "I got some fake documents, just enough to get me by—a driver's license and a social security number. I knew how from hearing Dylan talk about some of his cases. Anyway, my grandma and I were close when I was little, back in England. She was my rock, so that's why I wanted to use her name. It wasn't until after she died that my parents sent me away to boarding school here in the US."

He made a face.

"They weren't bad people. They just didn't know what to do with a kid. The boarding school was them trying to provide for me in the best way they could." She shrugged. "I always suspected it was because of my grandma that they didn't do it sooner. I know I should have picked a totally random name, but I didn't think…" She flushed and trailed off.

Still, he could guess what she was going to say. She didn't think her husband paid enough attention to what she wanted or who she was to know her grandmother's maiden name. But he was a cop; presumably, he knew how to chase a trail.

"None of that matters now," Andre said. "What matters is we figure out how to turn the tables on him." He tried to keep his tone even, but he could hear the aggression in his voice when he said, "It's time for Dylan to be the one jumping at shadows."

She stared back at him, shadows beneath her eyes and a weary slump to her shoulders. "How are we going to do that?"

"It's time to call in reinforcements."

Chapter Five

These were *some* reinforcements.

Juliette actually had to work to keep her jaw from dropping as Andre opened the door and ushered in two men who couldn't look more different than him. He introduced them as his brothers.

"We're not blood related," Cole Walker, Andre's older brother, said.

Clearly, he'd misunderstood her gaping. Thank goodness. She wasn't sure what she'd been expecting, but two men equally as attractive as Andre hadn't been it.

Cole had about two inches on Andre, and with his pale skin, light blue eyes and reddish-blond hair, they were total opposites. Throw in Marcos Costa, the youngest brother, with his jet black hair and piercing bluish hazel eyes, and no one would ever pick any of them as brothers. And yet they acted more like family than anyone who shared blood with her.

And, as she'd learned in the past two minutes, they all worked in law enforcement. Andre, in the FBI; Cole, a police detective just like her ex-husband; and Marcos, a DEA agent.

Women probably saw them together at family outings and wanted to suggest a *Hot Men of Law Enforcement* calendar. Still, as attractive as his brothers were, it was just Andre who made her pulse jump whenever she stared at him.

Which made no sense, because they barely knew each other. Besides, she should have learned her lesson when it came to instant attraction.

"—not quite what we were expecting," Marcos said, humor in his voice, and Juliette realized that not only had she not been paying attention, but he'd been talking to her.

"Uh, sorry," she mumbled.

"Juliette had a long day," Andre said, earning inscrutable glances from his brothers.

Clearly, they both wondered why he was risking his career to help her. But the family loyalty ran deep, and they walked into Andre's living room without a word, plopping onto the chairs on either side of the couch.

"What weren't you expecting?" Juliette asked, trying to catch up.

"You," Marcos responded with a dimpled grin as he flung his arms over the back of the chair and got comfortable.

"Knock it off," Andre said.

Although Juliette wasn't quite sure what he meant, she could tell Marcos was trying not to laugh. Cole was giving him a brotherly warning look, but underneath it, he seemed amused, too.

She had the distinct feeling that she was either the butt of a joke she didn't understand, or Andre's brothers thought something more scandalous was happening between her and Andre than a simple felony. Abducting a federal agent at gunpoint was surely a felony, she thought, then tried not to dwell on it.

Andre sat on the couch, and since it was the only seating left, Juliette joined him there, sticking close to the opposite side. No need to tempt herself even further by getting within touching distance of Andre. But nerves still shot through her at his nearness.

She scooted even closer to the far side, shifting so the armrest would hide her weapon. She'd kept her arm strategically placed over the bulging pocket of her cardigan since Andre's brothers had arrived, but she was pretty sure neither of them had been fooled.

"So, what's the plan?" Cole asked. "Get us up to speed here."

When Andre explained the last few hours—glossing over her armed abduction—Cole seemed considerably less amused.

She fidgeted, not liking the idea of Cole and Marcos thinking poorly of her. Their opinions shouldn't matter, but it was obvious how close they were to Andre, and already *his* opinion of her had become very important.

The three men were silent for a long minute, until Marcos burst out, "What a bastard."

It took her a minute to realize he was talking about her ex-husband. A tentative smile bloomed.

"We start there," Cole said, nodding at Marcos as though he was agreeing with his brother's assessment.

Juliette's shoulders slumped and she hadn't realized until that moment how tense she'd felt through Andre's explanation. Although he'd painted it as though her word was all he needed, she'd had no idea what reaction to expect from Cole and Marcos.

Even her own parents hadn't just blindly believed her when she'd tried to ask them for advice. They'd insisted she must have misunderstood what was happening. Then, they'd gone back to their own lives in England and hadn't bothered to check back in with her. She wondered what they thought now, if they'd heard about her in the news during the three years since she'd disappeared, and tried to push down the guilt.

"Start where exactly?" Juliette asked. "I wish I did, but I don't have any proof of the payoff."

"Well, technically, you do. Your eyewitness testimony," Cole said. "But that's not actually what I meant. I think we should investigate this attempt on your life. These cons took a payment for it, right?"

Andre nodded.

"So, there's a trail. We just need to find it."

"How?" Marcos asked. "We don't exactly have the legal authority to go for a warrant. This isn't our case. But I'm sure the Bureau will be doing that. What about Scott? Can he help?"

"I want to give him plausible deniability here," Andre replied. "He doesn't know Juliette came home with me. Right now, the FBI is searching for her. I don't want him to need to lie for me. Besides, HRT won't be handling the criminal investigation. That'll get handed off to the Washington Field Office."

"So, ask the WFO agents," Marcos suggested. "They'll share, won't they?"

"If they can find the money trail," Cole said. "But if these criminals don't even know who paid them, I'm betting it's pretty hidden. I know someone who can help."

"Shaye?" Marcos guessed, that same smile flickering on the corners of his lips that had been there when he'd spotted her in Andre's entryway.

"Yes, Shaye," Cole replied.

"You sure this isn't an excuse to see her again?" Marcos teased.

"Whether it is or not," Andre jumped in, "Cole is right." He looked at Juliette. "Shaye Mallory is some kind of computer forensics genius who used to work for Cole's department. If anyone can find a trail, it's her. Ask her," he told Cole. "But make sure she's careful. I don't want to spread it around why we're digging."

"Not a problem," he said, sitting a little straighter.

Even Juliette could tell he had a crush on this woman. The only question was why Shaye hadn't jumped at the chance to go out with him. She glanced between the brothers. The same was true of all three of them. What if Andre had a girlfriend? Maybe she'd misread his intent to ask her out when he'd saved her life in the woods this morning.

Wow, had it really been less than twenty-four hours since she'd been on her way to work, thinking everything was going to be normal today? Exhaustion hit so hard she couldn't stop herself from sinking into the cushions.

"I think that's our cue," Cole said.

"You take the big hardship and talk to Shaye," Marcos teased Cole, "and I'll start digging into the Manning murder, see if I can get any traction there."

"And I'll check into Dylan Keane," Andre said, a determined edge to his voice.

It wasn't until Andre stood to walk his brothers to the door that Juliette realized they were leaving because of her. She tried to sit upright again, get focused, but the stress of the day had finally caught up to her, and her body didn't want to obey.

"Thank you," she called after them.

Then Andre was back, scooping her off the couch as if she weighed nothing.

She squeaked—actually squeaked—with surprise and looped her arms around his neck for stability. He smelled vaguely of the woods he'd been running through this morning. On him, the scent of pine managed to be an aphrodisiac. Her voice came out breathy when she asked, "What are you doing?"

"Taking you to bed."

Suddenly, she wasn't tired at all. Her body came alive, sensitive to every inch of his arms looped under her back and knees, the solid warmth of his chest pressed against her side. She looked up to discover his face was much closer than she'd expected. If she just tilted her head back and snuggled closer, she could trace her lips over the adorable cleft in his chin, over the tiny dots of scruff just starting to come in, to his mouth.

Her throat went dry at the thought, and her pulse picked up until surely he could feel it. When his gaze met hers, his pupils instantly dilated.

She stared up at him, anxious for him to dip his head and kiss her but not wanting to break the anticipation. She let her gaze slide down to his lips and then back up to his eyes, so there was no mistaking what she wanted.

Some logical part of her was screaming a warning about the last time she'd taken a chance on a man in law enforcement, but logic was *not* winning against the desire in Andre's eyes. She could feel the pace of his breathing change beneath her, and his fingers curled into her arm and her leg where he held her. His head lowered, infinitesimally slowly.

Just when she was gripping his shirt to pull herself toward him, he straightened and picked up his pace, striding into a room and dropping her on the center of the bed.

Surprise made her laugh, then nerves kicked in. Kissing Andre was one thing, but she wasn't sure she was ready for anything more.

But he was already backing out of the room.

"You should get some sleep," he said, then disappeared through the doorway, leaving Juliette alone.

ANDRE SWORE UNDER his breath as he paced back and forth in the kitchen, forcing himself to stay away from the guest bedroom where he'd just deposited Juliette. He didn't know what had happened. Despite his attraction to her, his intent had been innocent when he'd picked her up. She was obviously exhausted. He'd planned to let her get some rest.

Then she'd stared up at him as if she wanted to devour him. The memory of it heated him until he opened his freezer and stood in front of it to cool down.

What was it about this woman?

Yes, she was gorgeous, but he knew plenty of beautiful women. And yes, he had a definite thing for a damsel in distress, but despite the challenges Juliette had obviously faced, she wasn't exactly screaming for someone to save her. The woman had stolen a gun off a federal agent, for crying out loud.

He squinted over at the couch where she'd been sitting and realized he hadn't imagined it. When he'd lifted her, the gun had dropped unnoticed out of her pocket.

Andre slammed the freezer shut, then walked over and picked it up. He went to empty the bullets and realized there were none. A startled laugh burst forth. Juliette had taken him hostage with an unloaded weapon.

He knew it had been loaded when she'd swiped it off Nadia at Quantico, which meant she'd purposely emptied it before holding it on him. He wasn't sure if that made the whole situation better or worse, but he took the gun into his room and locked it up.

Then he sank down on the edge of the bed, hearing Juliette toss and turn on the other side of the wall. He should have been polite and offered her a change of clothes to sleep in, a towel and some toiletries to take a shower. But he'd been too desperate to get out of there before he acted on their mutual attraction.

It was bad enough that he'd let her into his house and promised to help her evade the law. He didn't need to jump into bed with her, too. Because if he did, he'd get way too entangled. And no matter how much he might want to, he was still thinking logically enough to know it was a bad idea.

There wasn't a good ending here. Even if he helped Juliette prove her ex-husband was guilty, there was still the matter of her stealing Nadia's weapon and him hiding her from the FBI. If he got involved with Juliette, there'd be even more hell to pay.

As if on cue, his phone rang and the readout said it was Scott.

Andre didn't have to pick up to know why Scott was calling him back. Somehow, he'd figured out where Juliette had gone.

"I can explain," he answered the phone.

"Well, that's good, because Bobby said he thought he saw you on the freeway with this Juliette woman in your passenger seat."

Bobby was one of their friends on HRT, a monster of a guy who still managed to beat most of the team running the Yellow Brick Road at Quantico.

"I said that couldn't possibly be true," Scott continued, "because Juliette—or should I call her Mya?—was on the run, and the FBI was searching for her!"

"There's more to the story than you think."

"Well, there better be, because I don't think the FBI is going to appreciate one of their own agents hiding a fugitive."

"She was the victim," Andre reminded him.

"Until she took a weapon off a federal agent," Scott shot back.

Keeping her other illegal action under wraps,

Andre said, "She emptied the bullets. You'll probably find them in the parking lot."

"Great. She still stole the gun. What's going on?"

"I'm sorry I didn't tell you when you called before, but she's in trouble, okay?"

"So you gave her a lift off FBI property and hid her when you found out she'd snatched Nadia's weapon?"

"Not exactly. I'm just trying to help her. Her ex-husband is the cop who hired those goons to kill her."

There was a beat of silence, then Scott asked, "Can she prove it?"

"If she could prove it, do you think she'd be running?"

"Touché. Well, don't you think she's better off in FBI custody, where we can keep her safe?"

"I'm keeping her safe."

Scott swore. "This isn't exactly a career-advancing move you're making here."

"Yeah, I know."

"I mean, you could be in serious trouble. If she's in danger, the FBI will help her, but she can't just take an agent's weapon."

"Yeah, I got it," Andre snapped.

"I'm just trying to help you," Scott said softly. "What do you really know about this woman? Don't mess up your career for her."

Scott's argument was perfectly logical. Andre knew he was right. But still… "I can't walk away from her. She's totally alone, and she's got a cop gunning for her."

Although Andre had never found himself in her particular predicament, he did know exactly what it was like to be all alone in the world, and to feel as if the people who were supposed to help you had turned their backs. He'd gotten lucky, moving into the foster home with Cole and Marcos when he was nine. Before that, after his family had died, was a time he didn't want to think about too much.

The abuse had been sporadic. He'd think everything was fine, and then out of the blue, his foster father would knock him down the stairs. He'd tried to get help, but the person he'd told hadn't believed him, and he'd been too young to realize he should try again. Instead, he'd learned to be invisible.

Four years after he'd been put in that house, social services had gotten suspicious. They'd taken all the kids away, and Andre had been moved somewhere else. He'd expected the same thing, but instead, that very first day, Cole had somehow known what he'd been through. He'd told Andre that things would be different now, because he had a big brother to watch out for him.

The memories faded as Andre realized Scott had been saying something. "Sorry. What?"

There was an audible sigh on the other end of the line. "What can I do?"

"I was trying to keep you out of it. I don't want to mess you up here."

"Yeah, well, I should have realized earlier you avoided my question about whether you'd seen Juliette leave Quantico. I'm in it now. We're partners. I've got your back."

Andre smiled, knowing how lucky he'd been to have had Scott assigned as his partner. He'd gotten a whole new brother that day. "Thanks, man."

"Just try not to get us both kicked off the team for this, okay?"

Scott's tone was light, but Andre knew it was no joke. "We need to find the proof to connect her ex to the attempt on her life. And tomorrow, when I come in, I'll bring Nadia's weapon. I'll say I found it in the parking lot. It will be kind of true."

"You're coming in tomorrow?" Scott asked. "What about Juliette?" He paused. "Or do I call her Mya?"

"Juliette." Andre frowned. "Good point. I shouldn't leave her by herself. I doubt Keane could track her to my place, but I don't want to take any chances."

"Keane? That's his name?"

"Yeah. Dylan Keane. He's a cop out of Pennsylvania. She saw him take a payoff connected to the murder of Kent Manning."

Scott swore. "Okay, tomorrow I'll go see my fiancée and my sister at WFO, then use it as an excuse to drop in on the case agents, try to whisper that name in their ears and see what pops."

"I'm going to see what I can find from here."

"Good luck. And, Andre?"

"Yeah?"

"Try not to fall for this woman."

Too late. Instead of blurting his instant reaction, Andre replied, "I'll do my best. Thanks for the help."

Then he opened up his laptop. "All right, Dylan Keane. Time to dig up your skeletons."

Chapter Six

A soft *thud* woke Juliette from a deep sleep. She blinked, her heart racing, as she tried to get her bearings. She was lying under a soft blue coverlet in an unfamiliar room. For a minute, she panicked, until sleep cleared and she remembered. She was at Andre's house.

Everything was fine, she reminded herself. She tried to calm her pulse, which was still erratic, as if it knew something her brain didn't. Then she heard it again: another noise, this time a *thump*. Like someone was in the house. Someone besides Andre, whom she'd heard go into the bedroom, away from the noise, hours ago.

Judging by the darkness of the room, even with the shades partially open, it was the middle of the night. The sort of time someone would try to break in if they wanted to snatch her away while a federal agent slept in the next room.

"You're being paranoid," Juliette whispered

to herself, but she slipped carefully out of bed, stepping quietly toward the chair in the corner, where she'd left her cardigan.

She swore under her breath. When she'd taken it off, she'd realized the gun was no longer in her pocket.

Even if there were no bullets, it might have been a way to hold someone off, unless that someone happened to know she didn't like guns. She understood them, knew how to fire one, because Dylan had taught her. But they still made her nervous, and Dylan knew it. If her life depended on it, she wasn't actually sure she'd be able to fire at another person, even if she did have bullets.

Should she scream, try to wake Andre or his neighbors? If it *was* Dylan, what would he do? If he'd really sent hit men to kill her, would he be willing to take out anyone else who'd dare to help her? A shiver raced up her arms.

Dylan had caught up to her before, more than once. The first time, a month after she'd run, he'd come close. Way too close. He'd broken into her apartment in Cleveland in the middle of the night. Similar sounds had woken her up.

Her breath stalled in her throat at the memory. She'd barely slept in those first months, and every sound used to wake her. Which had turned out to be a good thing, because she'd slid out of bed and peeked around the corner, seeing him as he finally got the latch on her window open and began climbing into the apartment.

She'd run the other way, out the front door, leaving everything behind except her car keys as she leaped over multiple stairs at a time, trying to outrun him. He'd caught up to her on the second-floor landing. She rubbed her arm now, remembering the bruises he'd left behind.

Another *thump* and Juliette ripped herself out of her stupor. Two heavy bookends bracketed a handful of books on the dresser and she grabbed one of them, wielding it like a club in her shaking fist as she pressed up against the doorway, peering around the edge.

Her eyes adjusted slowly to the darkness as she slid down the hallway, pressed against the wall. Directly ahead, ominous shapes in the living room came into focus: the couch, the chairs, the table with all of Andre's pictures. Her attention was drawn to the window. Closed. No telltale fluttering of the curtains.

A faint creak drew her attention to the room beyond the living area. She hadn't been in there, but she knew it was the kitchen, because that's where Andre had gone when he offered to make everyone coffee yesterday. His brothers had both looked at her and frantically shaken their heads, and Andre had grumbled about his coffee being just fine.

Another creak, followed by something sliding across the floor. Someone was definitely in there, and now footsteps were moving toward her. Slowly, as though the person was trying to be stealthy. She never would have heard it if she hadn't been so close, listening so carefully.

Juliette pressed herself against the wall and lifted the bookend over her head, praying it wasn't Andre she was about to bash with the heavy marble piece. But then, why would Andre be sneaking around in the dark in his own house in the middle of the night?

She held her breath as the footsteps moved a little closer. Then, a figure darted through the doorway and had her pinned to the wall before she could swing the bookend. Her panicked breath caught in her throat and her pulse skyrocketed.

She squirmed, shoving herself forward, frantic to escape and torn between screaming for Andre and keeping him out of danger.

"Juliette. Juliette, it's me."

She looked up, into Andre's deep brown eyes, filled with concern and understanding, and embarrassment heated her. Along with intense awareness.

He was pressed against her, barely any space

between them from head to bare feet. His hands held her wrists against the wall behind her. He'd changed from the cargos and T-shirt he'd been wearing earlier into a pair of pajama pants and nothing else.

Every breath she took put even less space between them, and she was overly aware of how thin her camisole was, and grateful she hadn't slipped out of her bra before climbing back into bed. His bare skin brushed her arms, surprisingly soft over the steel of his muscles.

"Juliette," Andre said again, but this time his voice was almost a growl, and she watched the worry in his eyes turn into something more carnal.

"I thought you were an intruder," Juliette said. Her own voice sounded way too high and breathy.

"I know." A smile lifted his lips, then slowly faded. His grip on her wrists loosened, and he took the bookend from her, dropping it on the carpet with a heavy *thud*.

"I was working in the kitchen." His gaze slid slowly over her face, almost a caress. "I hit the lights, planning on a quick power nap, but I guess I really fell asleep. I knocked over a couple of things, and it woke me up. Then, I heard you and—"

"And you decided to sneak up on me?" She

tried to put some indignation into her voice, because he'd scared her, but it was hard to focus on being annoyed when she was working so hard not to loop her free arm around his neck and press her lips to his.

"Honestly, for a minute there, I wasn't sure it was you, the way you were obviously trying not to be heard. I wasn't sure until I came around the corner."

"And then you thought you'd tackle me anyway." Juliette cursed inwardly at the way the words came out, more flirtatious than accusatory.

He smiled again, moving in closer until his breath whispered across her lips, making her shiver. One hand was still locked around her wrist, but he moved it up, threading his fingers through hers over her head. The other hand slipped around her waist, moving slowly, as though he was giving her every chance to tell him to stop.

Instead, she closed her eyes and met him halfway. Desire made her body tingle at the first touch of his lips. He brushed them over hers, again and again and again, until she was glad she was sandwiched between him and the wall because she wasn't sure she could hold herself up. She was letting him set the pace—it was what she was used to—but she couldn't take it any-more, all those slow kisses teasing her senses.

So, she pulled her hands free and ran them up his bare arms, gaining courage at the way goose bumps pebbled his skin under her touch. When she reached his neck, instead of throwing her arms around him, she kept going, bracket-ing his face with her hands, and ran her tongue over the seam of his mouth.

That was all the encouragement he needed, because suddenly his tongue was dancing with hers, and excitement skipped along her nerve endings. The hand that had been tangled with hers slid into her hair, stroking through it, then down over her neck and shoulder before head-ing back up. She thought they were as close as they could get with clothes on, but he moved in closer still, until she could feel every inch of him, could tell how much he wanted her, too.

She tensed as doubt set in. She'd never been with anyone besides her husband. And look how that had turned out.

Andre must have felt her panic, because he backed up. Not far, but enough to put air be-tween them. He lifted his mouth from hers and stared down at her, as though he was waiting for something.

"I—I'm sorry," she stuttered. "I don't know—"

"It's okay." He took a step back and she almost fell forward at the sudden lack of contact.

"I'm just— This is…"

"You don't need to explain," Andre said, still breathing as hard as she was. "I get it."

Somehow, she doubted that, but she kept silent. Once upon a time, she'd been sure of herself. Sure of who she was, of what she wanted out of life. She'd worked hard at those boarding schools she'd hated, earned herself a scholarship to a school with a great art program because her parents refused to pay for anything but their alma mater. She'd chased her dreams of making a name for herself as a painter single-mindedly until Dylan had swept into her life.

Then, somehow, she'd slowly lost sight of who she was, who she wanted to be, alongside Dylan. And these past few years running had still been all about him. She hadn't really thought about it—she'd been so focused on building a life as someone new—until this moment. Now it was as if she was waking up from a nightmare and trying to find her footing again.

When she didn't speak, just stood staring at him, her mind on how she'd let her life get so out of control, Andre finally said, "Maybe we should go back to bed."

His words made her want to throw caution aside and follow him to *his* bed, but instead she simply nodded. She started to move toward the hallway again when she remembered. He said he'd fallen asleep in the kitchen, working. "What were you working on?"

"Your ex-husband."

"What?"

"I was digging into his records to see if I could connect him to Manning or the attempt on you."

Hopeful, she asked, "Did you?"

Andre shook his head. "I'm sorry. On paper, your ex seems clean. As in, perfectly, spotlessly, ridiculously clean."

Disappointment made her shoulders slump. It might not have been Dylan sneaking through Andre's house, but he was here nonetheless, still controlling her life. One bad mistake from which she couldn't ever seem to break free.

"YOU'RE NOT GOING to be able to hide forever."

The words coming through Andre's phone instantly flashed him back to the dream he'd had two nights ago, right before he'd been called in to the hostage situation. Memories rose up, images he hadn't focused on in years, of him kneeling in the grass, held back by Cole as he screamed for Marcos. Those terrifying moments when the roof had caved in, then Marcos diving through a window and Cole flattening him to the ground, putting out the flames on his pajamas. The rest of them—his foster parents and the other foster kids in the house—all standing outside in disbelief, watching their home disappear in the fire and smoke.

Something was wrong with that memory. He tried to recall more details from that night eighteen years ago, a time he'd tried hard to forget. But something about it was bothering him, and for some reason, Scott talking about hiding had made him think of the fire. He frowned, bringing the memories into clearer focus, but Scott's insistent voice pulled him back to the present.

"Froggy isn't buying that you're sick."

"Why not?" Andre asked, insulted even though he should have felt guilty since it was a lie. He'd called off work today in order to stick close to Juliette, but Scott was right. There was only so long he could do that before he'd have to return to work, so they needed to move fast on her ex.

"Uh, how about the time you showed up swearing you could still rappel out of a helicopter with a 101-degree fever? You were practically delirious, but you were sure you'd be fine sliding out of a helicopter fifty feet in the air."

"It wasn't that bad," Andre mumbled.

"Or when you told Froggy you could go right back to work after busting up your ankle?"

"Hmmm."

"Yeah. You should have been a little less eager then, because he doesn't believe simple food poisoning would keep you away from work."

"He's not going to call me, is he?" Andre had no desire to lie to his boss twice—the first time, over an answering machine, had made him feel bad enough. Besides, Froggy was a human lie detector. If they actually spoke, he'd know for sure.

"No. I told him I'd convinced you not to come in for once, that the guys didn't want to be puked on. But I don't think he really bought it. And how long can food poisoning last anyway?"

"We're off for the weekend," Andre reminded him, "and I've got some vacation days coming."

"Just deal with this mess and get back here. This woman isn't worth losing your job over." Before Andre could reply, Scott said, "Froggy's headed my way now, so I've gotta go. I'll let you know what I hear from WFO."

"Thanks," Andre said and Scott hung up.

Andre was slower to set down his cell, his mind going back to that dream as he absently sipped the coffee he'd poured himself a few minutes ago. It was just after 8:00 a.m., but he'd been up for an hour and a half already and since it had been four before he'd gone to his room last night, he was feeling the lack of sleep today.

Juliette hadn't emerged from his guest room

yet, but he'd heard her tossing and turning most of the night, so he wasn't expecting to see her for a while yet. By the time she woke, he wanted to have better news than he'd had last night. Her ex may have known how to stay below the radar, but if he was crooked enough to take a payoff for murder, it was doubtful that was his first step over the line.

If he had really hired three ex-cons to kidnap and murder his ex-wife, there was a trail. And by now, he knew he'd failed and would either be heading to Virginia to try to remedy the situation himself or he'd be frantically trying to bury that trail as deep as he could. So, Andre needed to find it while it was still hot.

"Morning."

Andre looked up at the soft, sleepy voice and found Juliette standing beside him, still wearing the dirt-covered slacks and camisole. Her hair hung in waves down her back, making him want to bury his hands in it, and her eyes were a little unfocused, the way they'd been last night after he'd kissed her.

Realizing he was staring, Andre jumped to his feet and grabbed a cup. "You want some coffee?"

"Uh, sure. Black is good. Thanks."

He poured her a big cup and handed it over, watching as she took a dainty sip and then cringed.

"Sorry. I make it a little strong."

"Yeah, like motor oil," she joked, but she took another drink, this one bigger, and joined him across the kitchen table.

The moment felt strangely domestic and intimate, as if they sat across the breakfast table together every morning. Stranger still, that idea felt somehow right.

He tried not to panic and pushed the thought aside. He couldn't fall for this woman. As soon as they figured out how to pin the attempt on her life to her ex, she'd be answering to the FBI herself. Granted, given the circumstances—if they could prove it—he was sure he could convince them to let her theft of Nadia's weapon slide. But then she'd be free. And somehow, he doubted she'd be returning to the life she'd built here—the little cubicle in the marketing company and the apartment where she'd planned to leave everything and run. She'd be gone, probably back to Pennsylvania, back to the life she'd left behind before she'd married Keane.

And he'd never see her again.

"What's the plan for today?"

Her words made him shake off his morose thoughts and focus on the immediate problem.

She seemed wary, as if she wasn't sure they could really stop her ex, and he didn't blame her, after being on the run for three years. But there was hope in her eyes, too, and the weight of her expectations hit him.

The responsibility to victims was something he was used to, usually in an immediate life-or-death situation, but this was a different kind of pressure. The pressure to help her, not to let her down. Even if it meant that as soon as he succeeded, she'd disappear from his life as fast as she'd entered it.

"You hire three ex-cons for a hit, and it doesn't matter how hard you try to bury it, there's still a trail. We're going to find it."

He could see her forcing herself to look optimistic, but her voice betrayed her. "He's a cop. He's handled too many investigations to screw up. He's not going to make a mistake."

"There's no such thing as the perfect crime, Juliette. I've handled a lot of investigations, too, and I promise you this: I'm going to bring him down."

Chapter Seven

Two hours later, after Juliette showered and tossed her clothes in his washing machine, Andre sat across from her, trying to focus. But with her so close—in a borrowed T-shirt and boxers, with damp tendrils of hair falling out of the knot on top of her head—all he could think about was leaning across the table and picking up where they'd left off last night.

"What?" Juliette asked, fidgeting and making him realize he was staring.

"Sorry. You're cute in my clothes." She smelled good, too. She'd used his soap. Although he didn't think it had any scent on him, on her it was sexy.

She blushed, and he couldn't help it. He had to tease her a little more. "So I have to know. How *did* you get the gun off Nadia? I mean, she's the agent they use at the Academy when they want to scare the NATs."

Juliette's forehead creased. "Gnats?"

"NATs. New Agents in Training. Nadia can get someone in a chokehold in less than thirty seconds." She was fast, and even though she had the sort of muscles that warned you not to mess around, most agents figured they were just as well trained and could hold their own. "I know, because it's happened to me."

Juliette leaned forward, propping her chin in her hands, and grinned at him. "Really? Now, that, I would have enjoyed seeing."

"Maybe I need tips from you." He leaned forward, too, until there wasn't much space between them and the amusement on her face turned into awareness. "How'd you do it?"

She shrugged, looking a little embarrassed. "It's not really that impressive. I don't think Nadia knew I was even there when she came in. She was changing in the stall, and the holster fell close to the edge of the doorway. I just slid the gun out and left the room before she realized it was gone. I'm not even sure why I took it, except I was feeling desperate to get out of there before Dylan showed up and told the FBI some story to take me with him. You know I never would have—"

"Fired on me with no bullets?"

She leaned back, and he wished he'd kissed her while they'd been inches apart. "You knew?"

"Not until you left the gun on the couch and I checked it. But I appreciate the fact that you weren't holding a loaded gun on me."

"And yet, you took me back to your house before you realized. Why?"

He shrugged. "I could see you needed help." He could tell she was going to press for more, so he added, "Besides, in HRT, we're trained to take down people holding weapons. I didn't view you as a particularly big threat."

Her lips pursed, as if she was trying to decide whether or not to be insulted, and then she sighed. "I guess you had the right instinct. I don't like guns."

"And yet you seem to know a lot about them."

"Dylan taught me. The first time he took me to the range, I think he just wanted to show off and impress me. Then he realized how much I hated shooting and he kept making me go back, said I needed to learn to be comfortable around them. He probably regrets that now."

Andre kept his opinion of her ex to himself. "Let's make him regret ever underestimating you." The words came out with a lot more vehemence than he'd intended.

She fidgeted again, as though she wasn't sure how to handle having someone on her side, and when she spoke again, she changed the subject.

"I've been thinking about something you said earlier, and it's been bothering me."

"Okay. Lay it on me."

"You asked me why Loews would take the fall for both him *and* Harkin over Manning's death. Why wouldn't Loews turn in Harkin if they were both guilty? And I don't know."

"Well, if you're right and they *were* in on it together, my guess is Harkin had something on Loews to keep him quiet."

"Something worse than a murder charge?"

"I meant, he was holding something over the guy. Probably a threat to his family."

Juliette asked slowly, "Do you think Harkin could have done the same thing to Dylan?" She fiddled with the edge of his T-shirt, not quite meeting his eyes. "You think Harkin told Dylan to either take the money and keep quiet or he'd hurt Dylan's family?"

When Andre didn't immediately answer, she looked up at him and then shook her head. "You think I'm naive, don't you? I mean, he tried to kill me."

"You married him. Whatever your feelings are now," Andre said carefully, "you loved him once. I get that."

And he did understand it. He didn't have to like it—especially any residual feelings she might have for the man she'd married—but he definitely got it.

She frowned. "This isn't me trying to make excuses for him. I don't want that life back. I just… I guess I'm trying to sort out in my head if he was ever the person I thought he was, or if I misjudged him from the very beginning."

"I'm sure—" Andre started, but she cut him off.

"This isn't really so much about him as it is about me." She pushed back the chair and stood, pacing in her bare feet across his kitchen. "We were only married for a year. And we didn't date that long, either. I met him about a year out of school. I've been running from him now for longer than I knew him. But the thing that bothers me most about it isn't so much that my ex-husband wants me dead."

She let out a humorless laugh. "Well, maybe it is. But how do I know if I can trust my own judgment about anything anymore? It feels as if it's not only him chasing me, but my own bad choices."

Andre slowly got to his feet, walking over to where she'd stopped and slumped against the wall. "You can't think that way. This isn't your fault."

She threw up her hands. "Maybe it is. I married the guy."

"That doesn't make you responsible for his bad decisions. Some people are really good at fooling others." He threaded his hand through hers, in part because he wanted to comfort her and in part because he'd liked the way her hand had felt in his the other night. "You're not to blame because he's manipulative. Trust me on this."

She stared down at their linked hands. "How?" she asked quietly. "How do I know I'm not going to let the same thing happen all over again?"

"I don't know," he said softly, because how could anyone guarantee they'd never trust the wrong person? "But you can't let one bad experience stop you from living your life. It's not fair that you've been running from your life because of him. We're going to get it back for you."

Juliette looked up into Andre's eyes, so full of conviction, and she couldn't help herself. She stood on her tiptoes and pressed her lips to his. He tasted like the horrible coffee he'd made that morning, mixed with something sweet and addictive she was already coming to associate as being uniquely *Andre.*

For a minute, he was still, not kissing her back. But then she moved in closer and he growled in the back of his throat and settled his hands on her hips, pulling her flush against him. The sudden full-body contact reminded her that she wasn't wearing anything underneath his boxers and shirt, and from the way he slanted his head and kissed her even more deeply, he'd felt it, too.

She locked her arms around his neck, trying to lift herself up even higher to eliminate the four-inch height difference between them. Then, the hands on her hips shifted lower and in one smooth motion, he lifted her, and her legs seemed to wrap around his waist without conscious thought.

The friction of his cargo pants against her bare thighs, along with his hands stroking over her hips, sliding under the edges of her shorts, made her whimper with a need she hadn't felt in a long time. His mouth migrated from hers to the side of her neck, nipping his way down to her collarbone until her head fell back. Then, his lips were back on hers and he was carrying her down the hall.

Instead of dropping her on the bed the way he'd done the other night, he laid her down slowly, settling on top of her and kissing her leisurely, as if they had all the time in the world. As if this were something real, instead of them being thrown together temporarily. In a flash of insight, she realized this *could* have been something real, if she'd met Andre under different circumstances. If she'd never made the mistake of marrying Dylan, never made such a mess of her life. Of course, then she never would have met Andre at all.

Andre lifted his head. "Where'd you go just now?"

"Sorry." She tried to tug him back down, but he stayed where he was, watching her. She stroked her fingers over the smoothness of his scalp, down over the bunching muscles in his back, and twined her legs with his. "I was just wishing we'd met under different circumstances."

"Me, too." He propped himself up on his elbows and gave her the half grin he used whenever he was about to tease her. "So, if we'd met differently, how do you think it would have happened?" He tipped his head to the side, as though he was thinking hard. "I bet you would have hit on me at the grocery store."

She let out a surprised laugh. "No way. You would have hit on *me*. And I doubt it would have been at the grocery store."

"Why's that?"

"Do you cook the same way you make coffee?"

"Hey!" He tickled her, and trapped underneath him, she squealed. "That'll teach you to make fun of my culinary skills."

"Oh, yeah?" She stroked her foot up and down

his leg, and skimmed her hands up underneath his shirt, until the smile dropped away and his gaze turned hungry. "You make terrible coffee," she whispered, stretching up to drop kisses on his chin and mouth. "Really bad."

"Okay. You can be in charge of making the coffee."

"That's not—"

He didn't let her finish, just molded his lips to hers, until all thoughts of teasing him disappeared. She shoved her hands up higher, tugging his shirt with it, until he helped her toss it aside. Then she was tracing her fingers over the muscles on his chest and abs, and hooking her legs up higher, around his hips.

Andre traced a line of kisses from her lips up to her ear, then whispered, "I must have had a great pickup line, wherever I was."

Juliette laughed, a lightness in her that she hadn't felt in years. "I guess so," she said, then fused her lips back to his.

A sudden vibrating on his leg startled her and he reached down and pulled out a phone, sighing and rolling off of her when he saw the readout. "Give me just a minute," he told her, then put on his serious voice and answered, "Scott. What's up? Tell me Froggy isn't on his way to my house right now."

"Froggy?" she mouthed, but he just grinned

at her. His look turned pensive as he listened to whatever Scott was telling him.

"And they don't know who it was?" A pause. "Did they run the number?" Another pause. "Huh. Okay, keep me updated if you hear more. Thanks, man."

Juliette sat up, tucking her knees to her chest and wrapping her hands around them as a bad feeling settled in her gut. She waited until Andre hung up, then asked, "What happened?"

"Scott had his fiancée talk to the case agents investigating the hit on you."

Juliette shivered at the terminology he used, so nonchalantly calling it a *hit*, and reminding her of what he did every day. The lust that had been warming her faded, leaving her cold. "What did they say?"

Andre slid next to her, leaning against the headboard, and tucked her under his arm. "A case with this kind of media attention, and the FBI always gets phone calls from citizens claiming to have information. We have to sort through it all, but most of the time it's nothing. But the agents got a call this morning from someone who was more interested in you than the hostage situation."

She wanted to ask if the agents had given out information about her, but they didn't know where she was, couldn't suspect she'd be here, so instead she asked, "They think it was Dylan?"

"They don't know anything about Dylan, remember? We're trying to drop the name with them, but we need to do it in a way that doesn't send them right to my door."

"Okay, so what are they doing about it?"

"There's not a lot they can do. The number went to a burner phone, so they don't know who made the call, other than it was a man and he asked about you specifically. He called you Mya."

Dread replaced the happiness she'd been feeling only a few minutes ago. "It's got to be Dylan."

"Probably. As far as we can tell, the media didn't get a hold of the name the cons had with your picture, and all your coworkers still know you as Juliette. None of them were told about it either."

"Do the agents know *anything* from this call?"

"Just that it came from Pennsylvania." He shifted to look at her. "I understand your reservations about trusting law enforcement, and believe me, I want to help you. But we're hindering our own investigation here. The best way to prove this was Dylan is to use all the FBI's resources. Which means turning yourself in."

Chapter Eight

"No way!" Juliette lurched off the bed and away from Andre.

He got up more slowly. His hands were out, as though he was trying to seem nonthreatening, but without his shirt, he looked like too many kinds of threats. "I know—"

"If you don't want to help me, fine. But I'm *not* turning myself in."

Andre sighed. "Juliette, the FBI won't let anything happen to you."

"Right." She turned and strode down the hall, into the small laundry room off his kitchen. She pulled her clothes out of his dryer, happy to discover they were mostly dry. "They'll say, 'no, of course it's not a big deal that you stole one agent's weapon and took another one hostage. Of course we're not going to arrest you for that. Of course we won't hand you over to someone else in law enforcement, who's got a spotless record!'"

She took a deep breath, knowing she sounded hysterical, and hugged her clothes to her chest. She wasn't about to strip naked and change in front of him. Funny how only a few minutes ago, she'd been desperate to get both of their clothes off. "If I go to the FBI, he'll find me."

"Not if you tell them what you saw," Andre replied, standing in the doorway with his arms crossed over his chest, effectively blocking her exit.

"Andre, I appreciate that you believe me, but you said it yourself. On paper, my ex appears perfect. And I…*don't.* I can't take the chance, okay? If you need me to go, then I will, but I can't turn myself in."

Memories flooded, of the humiliation she'd felt the day she'd gone into Dylan's station while he was out on a call. The looks the other officers had given her when she'd come out of the chief's office, half pitying, half disgusted. The way the chief had called out to have one of them "make sure she got home okay," as though she was incapable of driving herself. And then the way Dylan had glared at her when he'd come home that night. The fury on his face had been unlike anything she'd ever seen, telling her she had to get out before he killed her.

"Okay," Andre said softly.

She nodded, staring at the ground and trying not to tear up. She'd been alone a long time. She'd only known Andre for a little over twenty-four hours. He'd made her feel safe, as though she had someone she could rely on, someone she could trust, way too quickly. But she could do this on her own again. She'd run. She'd just have to keep moving this time, not stay in one place so long. "If you need to tell them I was here, please just give me a head start."

His arms went around her before she'd even realized he'd moved closer. "We'll do it ourselves. It'll be harder this way, but you've got a lot of people on your side. We'll figure it out."

"What?" She stared up at him in disbelief.

"You really think I'd let you go it alone?"

Her eyes stung, this time from tears of relief, but she blinked them back. Just because Andre was on her side didn't mean it was over. Dylan knew she was in Virginia now. Since the FBI hadn't given him any information, he'd start searching himself. And although she'd seen Andre in action and knew he was good at his job, Dylan hadn't gotten to be the city's top detective by accident.

Andre hugged her closer. "But just for the record, the Bureau is a good place, and we've got solid investigators. They wouldn't turn you over to a cop that you claim tried to have you killed just because he wears the badge."

She nodded against his bare chest, not bothering to argue. She knew he believed what he was saying, but he didn't know how persuasive Dylan could be. Or how persistent.

It had been three years. Three years where she'd tried to stay under the radar, where she'd kept silent. But that hadn't been enough for him. He couldn't just let her go, trust that she was scared enough she'd never turn him in—though it was doubtful anyone would have believed her anyway. Instead, he'd kept coming after her, no matter how hard she attempted to disappear.

Her jaw tensed as she thought about all the towns she'd tried to start over in, all the towns she'd had to leave—some in the middle of the night, leaving everything behind again. Maybe Andre was right about one thing. It was time to stop running. It was time to make a stand.

She pulled back from Andre's embrace just far enough to look up at him again. "I know you think we're at a disadvantage without the FBI's resources. But you have something better than that. You have me. And I know Dylan. So tell me what you need to know, and let's get started. Let's end this."

"I'VE GOT BAD NEWS." Cole stood in the doorway, holding a box of pizza and a case of beer, looking apologetic.

Andre tried not to let the words discourage him any more than he already was. He and Juliette had spent the day tracking Dylan's activities, digging up anything they could find.

Andre's thinking had been that since Shaye was searching for the money trail to the convicts, his time was best spent hunting down some other way to get Dylan behind bars. It didn't matter to him how, just so long as the guy was locked up. Once they took care of that, they could focus on nailing him for everything else.

But all their searching had come to absolutely nothing. Either the guy was way too good at hiding his transgressions or he really hadn't stepped over the line, except with the Manning murder case.

"What is it?" Andre asked, stepping aside so Cole could join him, Juliette and Marcos in the living room.

"I don't think Keane is behind this."

"What?" Juliette leaped from her seat. "Of course he is! Who else would send a bunch of criminals to kill me? You think I make a habit of pissing off dirty cops?"

Andre shot her a glance, and she visibly took a breath. "Sorry," she told Cole, running a hand through her hair and pulling part of it out of the complicated knot she'd put it in earlier. "It's been a long couple of days."

In his typical way, Cole shrugged it off. "No worries. Here." He tossed her a bag.

She opened it. "Where did you get these?"

"Shaye said you'd need something to wear if you'd been in the same clothes since the shooting. I have no idea about sizes, so she just gave me stuff with drawstrings. You'll probably need to roll the sleeves though—she's pretty tall. And she sent sandals. She said you could adjust them."

Juliette looked so pleased that Andre mentally slapped himself for not thinking of it. They'd been cloistered in his house for two days, so he hadn't thought much of her going barefoot or wearing his T-shirts. In fact, he liked her best barefoot and in his T-shirts.

"What are you grinning about?" Marcos asked, but the way he was glancing from Andre to Juliette suggested that he already suspected the answer.

"Nothing." Andre got back to business. "What do you mean, you don't think Keane is behind this?"

"You know how good Shaye is, right?" Cole prompted as he set the pizza and beer on the coffee table and Marcos helped himself to a slice.

"Yeah, I remember." Last year, Cole had been involved in a dangerous investigation of a gang with a reputation of gunning for anyone who tried to take them down. Shaye had used her computer forensics skills to dig up a money trail no one else had been able to find, landing the leaders in jail. But not before they'd done a drive-by at the police station, killing several officers and driving Shaye out of police work.

"How'd you get her to help with this anyway?" Andre asked. He knew Cole had tried to get her to return to the department before with no luck.

"It took a lot of begging. But I think it's good for her. She loves the work. It's being at the station that's the problem. PTSD from the shooting. Anyway, she's still searching, but she's already tracked most of Keane's assets. He's definitely living above his means, but there's no trail of money going out. Not the kind of money you'd need to hire three ex-cons for a hit."

"So what does that mean?" Juliette asked. "You think maybe it was some different sort of trade? Maybe he wouldn't arrest them for something if they did this for him?"

Andre shook his head. "No. Both the perps in custody specifically talked about a payment. They got half beforehand and were expecting the rest after the job was finished. There's got to be a trail."

Cole shrugged. "Well, there's not. At least not going from Keane. Not even to some third-party account that these guys could draw from. She's still digging, but she says if she hasn't found it at this point, he'd have to be really skilled at hiding money. If she doesn't get any hits soon, she's going to try it the other way, from the criminals out, but it's going to take longer."

"Why?" Juliette asked.

"Because there are three of them, and she's doing it off-book," Marcos answered, without pausing as he devoured his slice of pizza. "She's got to cover her tracks. It's not as if she has a warrant for this. Not only is she not assigned the case, but she's a private citizen now."

"Oh." Juliette frowned and Andre could tell exactly what she was thinking.

"She won't get caught," Andre promised.

"But if she finds something, we'll have to find a way to give the trail to the case agents, so they can pull the information legally," Cole added. "We have to leave her name out of it. Right now, we're doing it to verify we're after the right guy and to know where to send them. But this won't put him away, because we don't have any jurisdiction here."

"And you guys are okay with this?" Juliette looked from one to the next. "Doing this outside the law?"

"Not really," Cole said, flopping onto one of the empty chairs. "But this isn't a regular thing. Andre wouldn't ask if there was another option."

Juliette fidgeted and then sat forward. "I don't want—"

"Besides," Cole spoke over her, using his big brother protective voice, "if someone in law enforcement had put a hit out on *my* girlfriend, I'd be doing the same thing."

He didn't seem to notice Juliette turning red, but Marcos was clearly trying not to smile at her reaction. Andre just hid his surprise that Cole thought Juliette was better off hiding in his house than under FBI protection. And that Cole had equated her to his girlfriend and already liked Juliette enough to get protective of her.

"I mean, I trust the FBI, and I'm sure they'd put you in a safe house, but they're still going to have to give a fellow law enforcement officer the benefit of the doubt, especially if there's no evidence to support your claim. If the guy knows he's under investigation, he's got the skillset to hide the evidence. And at some point, if they can't pull up any proof?" Cole shook his head.

"I'll be back in danger," Juliette said softly, as if she'd known that all along.

"That's not going to happen," Marcos spoke up before Andre could say the same thing.

"You don't even know me," Juliette said, looking genuinely perplexed. "Why are you doing all of this?"

"You matter to Andre," Marcos said simply, "so you matter to us."

"Thank you," she said softly, and his brothers must have been able to see as well as he could that she was overwhelmed, so both of them shrugged as though it wasn't a big deal and grabbed pizza.

But it was a big deal. And he knew it as well as Juliette. There weren't many people he'd ask his brothers to put themselves on the line for, and he'd known Juliette less than forty-eight hours. He wasn't sure how she'd become so important to him in such a short time, but he knew it was more than just a simple need to protect her.

He felt connected to her, on a level he didn't totally understand. But one thing he did know: he couldn't let anything happen to her.

Deciding to worry about what his feelings meant later, Andre took the remaining chair and popped open a beer. "Scott says the WFO agents got a call from someone digging for information about Juliette. We assume it was Keane, since it was a burner phone."

"Well, he could make the drive in an evening and be back before morning, but he'd have to know exactly where she was first," Marcos said.

"It'd be a stretch," Cole put in. "As a cop, he'd probably take back routes to avoid traffic cameras as much as possible, and that would add a lot of time to the trip. But you're right. He's not going to come out here without already knowing exactly where she was."

What neither of them was saying—and Andre wasn't about to either—was that if Dylan made that trip, it would be to kill Juliette and then drive back before anyone knew he'd left the state.

"The news was reporting our team was at the hostage situation, but he'd have a hard time getting names, even if he knew someone in the Bureau. And then he'd have to narrow it down to me and suspect I was harboring her," Andre said. "That's not going to happen."

"So, what's next?" Cole asked. "Marcos, did you find anything?"

Marcos shook his head and set down his third slice of pizza. "I wish I had more to report, but everything in the Manning investigation seems above board. Loews had motive, means and opportunity, and they found his prints at the scene. If Harkin was there with him, I can't find any sign of it."

"Maybe they both plotted it, but Loews was the actual killer," Cole suggested.

Juliette shrugged. "I don't know. What I heard was my husband—my ex—telling Harkin he'd keep his name out of it, but he couldn't do anything for Loews. About a week later, they arrested Loews, so I assume they already had evidence against him."

"What about Harkin? He was a suspect before that?" Cole asked.

"Oh, yeah," Juliette answered. "With Manning dead, Harkin took control of the company. It's worth millions of dollars. First, they ruled out Manning's wife—I'm told that's common practice with homicide. After that, Harkin and Loews were the next obvious suspects—his business partner and his biggest competitor."

"And Dylan Keane was the lead detective on the case," Marcos contributed. "He already had a great track record at the station, but this was his biggest case. Still, I'm not seeing any signs of impropriety. From what I can tell, Harkin *did* get investigated and cleared. So, either Keane made evidence against him disappear or…"

"Or what?" Juliette prompted.

"Or there wasn't any to begin with."

"Then why give Dylan a payoff?"

"Harkin wouldn't be privy to what evidence the police had. It's possible Keane took a gamble, told Harkin he could put him away and offered an alternative."

"But if Harkin was innocent, that's a big gamble."

"Not really," Marcos said. "Dirty or not, Keane was a good investigator. Even if he couldn't prove it, he probably knew Harkin was involved."

"Well, if there wasn't any evidence, then he's only guilty of taking a payoff." Juliette sounded dismayed. "Proving that isn't going to put him away forever."

"No, but proving he tried to have you killed will," Andre said.

Juliette nodded, and he could tell she was trying to look optimistic, but didn't feel it. He couldn't blame her. So far, their digging into Keane hadn't yielded anything. But years of working as a regular special agent before he'd transferred to HRT had taught him this kind of investigation rarely happened quickly. It took time. At least with Keane in Pennsylvania on the job, he wasn't here hunting Juliette.

Cole cursing brought Andre's attention back to his older brother. He was staring at his phone and then he shook his head, and he didn't have to say a word for Andre to know he had more bad news.

"Shaye just texted me. Don't ask me how she knows this, but Keane just put in for a week's vacation. Starting tomorrow."

They were all silent a moment, then Juliette spoke the obvious. "He's coming here. He's coming for me."

Chapter Nine

"Who do we know in Leming?" Cole asked.

"Leming, Pennsylvania?" Marcos replied.

"Yeah. Supposedly that's where Keane was going for his vacation, to a friend's cabin out there. I recognize that town. Why?"

"Kendry patrols near there," Marcos reminded him. He told Juliette, "A guy I worked a joint task force with about six months ago. He's a small-town cop, but he's got one of the best eyes for trouble I've ever seen. We tried to recruit him, but he preferred small-town living."

Juliette tried to focus. "Recruit him?" she echoed, her mind still reeling with the news that Dylan was on his way here. She knew he'd come eventually, of course, which was why she'd been trying to run in the first place. But being in Andre's house had begun to lull her into a sense of security.

"To the DEA." When she didn't respond, Marcos added with a lopsided grin, "That's where I work."

"Oh. Right." She sounded as dazed as she felt, and as Andre's brother got on a call with Kendry, all the decisions she'd made in her life that had driven her to this point flashed through her mind.

This was the first time in three years that she'd told anyone the truth about who she was and why she was running. This was the first time she hadn't felt totally alone. The truth was, she felt safer than she had in a long time, because she knew without needing to ask that any one of them would put himself in front of a bullet for her.

That thought filled her with a terror greater than her fear of Dylan. She looked at Marcos, talking animatedly on the phone while Cole huddled close to listen, his expression serious and intense. Then over at Andre, leaning forward, his elbows resting on his knees, a determined energy radiating from him.

When she'd held a gun on Andre and demanded he drive her out of Quantico, she'd never expected this. She hadn't thought it through, how it might impact him and his family. She'd just been fixated on her own next moment, living to see another day.

It was how she'd approached her life for the

past three years. Those years were just a blur of new cities, new states, new names. She'd made what could loosely be called "friends," but she'd never let herself get close enough to anyone that her past might come up. Never close enough to have to explain where she'd come from or how she'd gotten there. The whole time, she'd been going through the motions, never planning for a future she wasn't sure she'd have.

Now, suddenly, she wanted one. Desperately.

She mentally traced Andre's features: the strong profile, the furrow he got between his eyebrows when he was deep in thought, the little dimple when he gave her one of his sly grins.

As though he could sense her staring, Andre turned toward her, that furrow appearing. She ducked her head. She didn't want him to read her too closely now, because he'd see things she wasn't ready to admit yet, not even to herself.

She couldn't let anything happen to him because of her. That thought blared in her mind as if it was coming through a bullhorn.

"He's there."

She looked over at Marcos. "What?"

"Kendry didn't even have to check," Marcos said, sounding surprised. "He said Keane arrived in Leming an hour ago and actually stopped by the station, letting them know, one officer to another, that he was around."

Cole frowned. "That's a little unusual. You think he's trying to set up an alibi?"

"Maybe. But why there?" Andre asked. "It's not any closer to Quantico, and he's less likely to have people who can account for all his time. As alibis go, he'd be better off staying home and sneaking out and back during the night."

"True, but in Leming, he's got a potential alibi *without* so many eyes on his activities. Maybe that's the point," Cole suggested.

"The timing is too suspicious to be coincidental," Marcos agreed. "But at least we have a contact there. Kendry's going to try to keep track of him, let us know if he spots him leaving."

"So, what's next?" Cole asked, eyeing Juliette as though he suspected what she was beginning to realize. "Keane—legitimately or not—seems innocent, and Manning's murder investigation appears above board." He looked at Andre. "You didn't find anything else in Keane's record, right?"

"Nope." The single word was bursting with frustration.

"Any chance he spotted our tracks?" Marcos asked. "It might explain why he took off."

Cole slowly shook his head. "I doubt it. But it's possible. Which means maybe we need to consider a completely new alternative."

"What?" Juliette asked, not following.

Andre took one of her hands in his, either oblivious or uncaring of the look his brothers shared when he did it. "What if someone else put the hit on you?"

"No—" Juliette started, but Andre cut her off.

"Just consider it. You said Keane has been chasing you for years, but has he tried to kill you before? Or was he trying to drag you back home?"

Juliette remembered that moment in Cleveland when he'd caught up to her on the stairwell. Her panic as she ran out of her apartment in her bare feet and pajamas, so fast she'd almost fallen down the stairs. The sound of his boots pounding on the steps behind her. The feel of his hand as he'd gripped her arm so hard she'd worried he'd pulled it out of the socket. The bruises that hadn't gone away for a month.

This time, she focused in on that single moment when they'd stood in the stairwell together. She'd whipped around to face him, terrified. She'd expected to see a weapon in his hand or the same fury that had been on his face when he'd threatened to kill her if she ever told. But instead, there'd been desperation.

She hadn't waited to see what he'd wanted. She'd just screamed as loud as she could and been so grateful when two neighbors peered into the stairway almost immediately. He'd let go of her arm, and she hadn't looked back. She'd just run.

She'd kept what she thought of as her "escape bag" in her car, with a change of clothes, some money and forged documents for a quick getaway. She'd peeled out of town and driven for days, sleeping only occasionally on the side of the road, before driving again. She'd traveled through multiple states before she'd stopped that first time.

"I don't know," she admitted now. He'd caught up to her again, more than once, but she'd spotted him and run before he could get close. "But he threatened to kill me before I left if I ever spilled his secret."

Andre leaned closer. "But did you ever hear him say he'd planted evidence? Anything other than he'd keep Harkin's name out of it, but he couldn't help Loews?"

Juliette shook her head, wondering what he was getting at.

"What if we're going about this wrong?" Andre asked. "What if Keane wasn't the only one involved?"

"What do you mean?" Juliette asked, her mind spinning from the possibility that she might have been wrong about Dylan's plan in Cleveland. She'd never before questioned that he'd been trying to kill her. But what if he'd actually intended to grab her and drag her back home?

The longer they'd been married, the more possessive he'd become. Maybe he really didn't want her dead—just wanted her somewhere close so he could keep controlling her, make sure she wasn't a threat.

What difference did it make? Death or prison?

"It's a real possibility," Cole said, as if he could read Andre's mind. "Keane must have had a partner on the force, right?"

She nodded. "Yeah, of course. They'd been friends since childhood. They joined up together, were on patrol together, then got their detective shields together. Jim Valance. They were like brothers." She paled, as realization hit. "You think they were in on the cover-up together? That Dylan was trying to bring me home to protect me in his own stupid way, and that it's *Jim* who's trying to kill me?"

JULIETTE FELT AS though she had whiplash. Dylan was trying to kill her. Dylan *wasn't* trying to kill her. Dylan was guilty. Dylan was innocent—or at least, not *as* guilty. Jim was guilty.

Jim Valance. The first time Juliette had met him had been the day Dylan had pulled her over. Jim had been in the car with him. Then, later, when Dylan showed up at the club, Jim was there, too, playing wingman. A year later, he'd been Dylan's best man at their small wedding ceremony.

Why hadn't she ever considered that Jim might be involved? Juliette mentally kicked herself. It would certainly explain why Jim had been so furious when she'd come into the station to turn in her husband, his silent fuming when he drove her home. She'd assumed it was simple loyalty. She'd never thought she was putting Jim's career in jeopardy, too.

"Dylan used to talk to me about his cases sometimes," Juliette said, as three pairs of eyes, so different physically but so similar in intensity, focused on her. For the first time in years, she thought back to that first year with Dylan and remembered more than just the bad. "I remember when he got the Manning murder case. He was so excited because it was the most high-profile case the department had gotten in years, and his chief had made him lead."

"How did Valance feel about that?" Andre asked when she paused.

"I don't know. I saw Jim all the time, but there was always a little…I don't know, jealousy maybe?…between us. I think he felt as though I sort of took Dylan away from him. I figured he was happy for Dylan about the assignment.

I mean, they were partners, so that effectively made Jim one of the leads, too."

"But he wasn't the head detective," Cole said. "That might have been a sore spot."

"Maybe. But he never acted upset about it that I saw. But what I do remember, from early on in that case, is Dylan complaining about Jim. When they started the investigation, Dylan suspected Harkin."

"He talked to you about his cases a lot?" Andre asked.

"Sometimes." It was more like he talked *at* her about his cases. He hadn't really wanted her opinion about them. He'd just needed someone to listen silently while he worked things out aloud. She hadn't really minded back then, but in retrospect, it had been representative of a lot of things in their marriage. He'd wanted to be in control, to have her around when he needed her.

Back then, she'd thought that was love. Her parents hadn't hidden the fact that they hadn't planned to have her and didn't know what to do with her once they did. She'd avoided a lot of entanglements in boarding school. Then, Dylan had showed up and focused all of his attention on her.

It had never really occurred to her to wonder if he'd liked her for who she was or because he could mold her into what she wanted her to be.

And it had probably been so much easier for him to do it since she'd had virtually no support system. He'd chipped away at the rest, little by little, so slowly she hadn't realized it was happening, until all her friends were acquaintances.

Still, he wasn't all bad. She'd loved him once, and although she had memories of feeling lonely in their relationship, she also had memories of them laughing together when things were good and leaning on each other when times got hard.

"Juliette," Andre said softly, bringing her back on track, "when did Dylan stop saying he suspected Harkin? Was it after he took the money?"

"He stopped talking to me about the case at all around then. But before that, he complained about Jim. I'd forgotten all about it, because of everything that happened afterward, but initially, Dylan was mad because Jim kept insisting Harkin was innocent." She frowned. "Actually, I think it was Jim who first suggested Loews was a better bet than Harkin as the killer."

"What if *Jim Valance* tampered with evidence rather than Keane?" Cole suggested. "Harkin could have approached Valance first, offered him money to lead the investigation away from him and toward Loews. But Valance couldn't convince Keane that his theory on Loews was right, so Harkin decided to pay Keane off, too."

"It would explain why you just heard your ex

talking about keeping Harkin out of the investigation and not about making any evidence disappear," Marcos agreed. "Maybe Valance already told Harkin that he could only do so much—it might have been easier to hide the evidence that Harkin was there than it would have been for both of them."

"Did Valance know you'd overheard your ex and Harkin talking?" Andre asked.

"I don't think so. I don't think he realized I knew Dylan had taken money until I showed up at the station to report Dylan."

Andre stroked the hand he'd been holding since they'd first started this discussion. "Those times you spotted Keane tracking you when you were running from him—did you ever see anyone else? Did you ever see Valance?"

Juliette frowned, focusing on those days in Cleveland before Dylan had showed up in the middle of the night. She thought of the day she'd spotted him talking to someone in the tiny town she'd moved to in Arkansas, and the time she'd seen him coming out of the post office in the spot she'd picked in Maine. She thought hard, trying to remember if she'd ever noticed anyone else, but finally she had to shake her head. "If Jim was with Dylan, I never saw him."

"If we're right about this," Marcos said, "he wouldn't have been with Keane at all. He would have been either ahead of him or behind him, trying to track you down first."

"What about the ex-cons who showed up at your job?" Cole asked. "Did you recognize any of them?"

She shook her head. "I figure Dylan arrested them at some point or another. They had arrest records from our town."

"And if Valance was his partner…"

"Then Valance was in on those arrests, too." She dropped her head to her hands, feeling Andre's strong fingers beneath her cheek, too. "I can't believe I just assumed it was Dylan all this time, when it was actually Jim."

"It's just a theory," Cole reminded her, but she could hear in his voice that he thought they were on the right track.

She lifted her head and looked from one brother to the next, stopping on Andre. "So, if Jim sent those hit men after me, and Dylan is hiding out in Leming right now, does that mean Jim is gunning for both of us?"

"I don't know," Andre replied. "It's possible. Announcing to the locals that he's there could be Keane's way of giving himself protection. He goes out of town and gets killed and his partner is also away, the partner's an obvious suspect. But the two of them on a job together, day after day? It would be too easy for Valance to set up an ambush."

Juliette shivered, and she knew Andre saw it. She didn't want to go back to Dylan, but she didn't want him dead, either. "So, what do we do now?"

Andre and his brothers started talking strategy, but Juliette didn't hear any of it. Because she suddenly knew the answer.

It didn't matter who was after her. What mattered was that these men had vowed to protect her. They'd put their careers on the line to help her, and she didn't doubt they'd do the same with their lives. And she couldn't let them make that sacrifice.

It was time for her to go.

ANDRE OPENED HIS eyes slowly. The sun was already streaming through the slats in his blinds as fragments of his dream came back to him. He'd been dreaming about the fire again, and it had woken him repeatedly during the night, then he'd fallen back into fitful bits of sleep. Every time he'd woken, he'd thought about getting up and walking into the room next door, where Juliette slept. But he'd resisted.

She'd handled the news that maybe her ex-husband hadn't been out to kill her for the past three years surprisingly well. But he'd also seen the regret on her face that she'd misjudged him. Maybe even wistfulness for what they'd once shared.

The idea that she might still love her ex-husband made his chest hurt. But he had no claim on her. He'd only known her a few days. It wasn't enough time to form a genuine bond with someone. Or at least that's what he'd told himself every time he'd woken up last night. But the truth was, he felt more connected to her than he'd ever felt to another woman, logical or not.

He identified with how alone she'd found herself, because he'd been there. And he admired how she'd forged forward on her own, using her wits and intelligence to not only survive but to build a new life for herself in each new town. She was a fighter, just like him. And this was a battle he was going to make sure she won.

He noticed the silence in his house and looked over at his alarm clock. He'd slept later than usual. When he sat up, more pieces of his dream returned, and he swore. The thing that had been nagging him about his memories of the fire had surfaced in his dreams.

The sun had been coming up that morning, too, but instead of 9:00 a.m., it had been sunrise. Well before anyone in that house woke up. Everyone should have been coming from upstairs that morning, fleeing through the front door or the side. And yet, his foster father and one of the other foster kids had come around from the back of the house. Why?

The house had burned down that day. The foster family had been totally split up, and he'd never seen those parents or the kids, other than Marcos and Cole, ever again. But years later, he'd seen the report about the fire.

It had been deemed an accident and he'd never questioned that before, because supposedly the firefighters had found candles left burning. Andre had assumed his foster father had forgotten to put them out before going to bed. But the fire had started near the back of the house.

For the first time, he suspected someone had started that fire on purpose.

The idea sent fury and sadness and a hint of fear running through him. Who? And why?

He threw his covers off and stood and it struck him again how silent the house seemed. Was Juliette still asleep?

A new dread crept up on him and he strode into the next room in nothing but his boxers, flinging open the door. But the room was empty, the bed neatly made. And he knew it even before he walked through the rest of the house.

Juliette was gone.

Chapter Ten

"You need to get down here *now*," Scott told him when Andre fumbled to pick up his cell phone as he was climbing into his car.

The car that thankfully Juliette hadn't taken with her. Which meant she'd either walked wherever she was going or gotten a cab.

He didn't like the idea of either one. What was she thinking, sneaking out on her own when someone was searching for her, trying to kill her? Regardless of whether it was her ex-husband or his partner, someone still wanted her dead. And she was giving them a much easier target.

No one would know to search for her from his house, Andre told himself as he belatedly answered Scott. "Get where now? Where are you?"

"At Quantico."

"You are? Why?" They had the weekend off.

"I came in to pick up some gear I left. And

you're lucky I did, because guess who's at the entrance gate right now, turning herself in?"

Andre swore. "When did she get there?" And what the heck had she been thinking?

"Just now. I was on my way out when I saw the cab pull up and she climbed out. Either she admitted to taking the gun off of Nadia or they suspect she's involved in something herself, because they've got her in cuffs right now."

"She's not armed," Andre said, starting his car and racing out of his drive. "I have Nadia's gun, minus the bullets."

"Yeah, *I* know that," Scott said, "but you really want me explaining to the guard at the gate that you've had possession of an agent's stolen weapon for two days? If Juliette was going to turn herself in—which I think is a good idea, incidentally—this isn't exactly the best way to do it. You need to be careful how you play this, or you're going to be facing an OPR investigation."

That was probably going to happen no matter what. But he'd known it from the moment he'd agreed to help Juliette. The FBI's Office of Professional Responsibility was going to want to review his actions. If he was lucky, it would be a mark in his permanent file. He didn't want to think about what would happen if he was unlucky.

"Just get over to the gate," Andre said. "Tell

them to wait for me before they talk to her. I'm coming in now."

"Yeah, well, step on it," Scott replied. "I'm—"

Whatever he was going to say next was cut off by the sound of a *bang, bang, bang* Andre would recognize anywhere. Shots fired.

"Scott? What's happening?" Andre asked frantically, but the call disconnected.

Andre stepped on the gas.

SOMEONE WAS SHOOTING at her. And they were doing it at an FBI facility!

Juliette pushed aside her disbelief and dropped to the ground, trying to absorb the weight with her hips and shoulders since her arms were cuffed behind her back. Pain ricocheted through her body, but adrenaline pushed her on. Awkwardly, she scooted toward the guard post, but her too-small sandals snagged the hem of the too-long pants Shaye had lent her, slowing her down. All around her, more weapons went off— she assumed agents firing back.

She had no idea who they were shooting at, because she couldn't see anyone. But she recognized the sound of a rifle, which meant the shooter probably had high ground.

How could Jim have possibly tracked her here? It didn't make any sense, unless he'd been watching Quantico, waiting for her to show up because the news had reported that HRT agents had responded to the hostage situation. But that seemed far-fetched. Maybe the shooting was random, not aimed at her.

Another rifle shot fired amidst the pistols. Pain exploded in her leg and she screamed, any doubt gone. This was about her.

She tried to wriggle into the guard post, out of the line of fire, but before she could go anywhere, a figure leaped into her line of sight, yanking her off the ground and practically tossing her behind the booth. Then she was squashed against it, her wrists burning from the handcuffs and her lungs compressed by a man's back against her.

For a minute, new panic made her desperate to move. Was she exposed here, standing up? Was he? But he seemed to know what he was doing, and as he turned his head and scanned the tree line to the left just as another rifle shot fired, she realized who he was. Andre's partner from the day they'd met.

"Muzzle flash, my seven o'clock," he yelled, and then a new barrage of shooting began. "Whoever is outside the shooting zone, flank him!"

"We've got agents heading there now," the guard in the gatehouse yelled back. "More on their way."

She'd done this, Juliette thought, praying no one had been hit. Besides her, she realized, remembering the flash of intense pain in her leg. She couldn't feel it now—her adrenaline was pumping so hard—but she could stand, so she figured it couldn't be too bad.

"He's after me," Juliette told the agent protecting her. Scott, she remembered. His name was Scott.

"It's his unlucky day, then," Scott replied, his tone hard and too calm. "Because now we're after him."

She prayed he was right, that they'd catch him, and no one would be hurt because of her. She'd come here today because she couldn't bear the thought of Andre or his brothers getting hurt—physically or facing professional consequences—because of her. If her actions caused someone else to be shot, she didn't think she'd ever forgive herself.

Tears pricked her eyes. No matter what she did—run or hide or take a stand—it never seemed to end. He was still after her. Whether *he* was Dylan or Jim, or both of them—she didn't know.

Her eyes dried, and anger hit. She hadn't done anything wrong—at least not until her misguided attempts to get away from Quantico. Someone else had set all of this in motion, chasing after her when she would have kept her silence and stayed hidden. Maybe it was time to really stand up and fight. To finally end this.

If only she knew how.

"Andre's almost here," Scott said and Juliette realized she had no idea how much time had passed.

It felt as if it had only been a few minutes since the shooting started, but if Andre was close, that wasn't possible. How long had they been standing here, pressed against the guard booth, avoiding bullets?

The shooting had stopped, she realized. The air around them was quiet, too still after all the gunshots. "What happened? Did anyone get hit?"

"Everyone is okay. Unfortunately, though, the shooter got away," Scott said. "But he made himself a hide up there. He's been there before, so there's a trail. Plus, we've got his casings. We'll get prints. And then there's nowhere this guy will be able to hide. He shot at federal agents, which tends to piss us off. He's going down."

She tried to move, to squirm out from behind Scott and look at her leg, but he pushed her back.

"You're not going anywhere until I have the hundred-percent all clear. Sorry."

"I'm sorry," she whispered back, but she didn't think he'd heard her, because by then he was talking into a phone and then he was finally letting her move.

But as soon as he stepped away, she almost fell. She steadied herself, hoping he hadn't noticed, but then he was saying into the phone, "By the guard booth. Get over here. I think she was hit."

Juliette looked down, almost in a daze as she watched Scott take out a tactical knife and slice open the side of her pant leg, which was ripped and blood splattered. He poked at her leg, making her jerk away.

"False alarm," he said, standing again and addressing her while talking into the phone. "A bullet must have hit close to you. It kicked up concrete. It's not going to be fun to have the pieces pulled out of your skin, but there's no bullet wound. You're okay. Turn around," he added, and when she didn't immediately move, he turned her and then she felt the handcuffs click open.

She rubbed her raw wrists and nodded her thanks.

"Got it," Scott said into the phone. Then he held out the phone to her. "Andre wants to talk to you." His tone practically sing-songed, *you're in trouble.*

She made a face at him and he laughed. How he could laugh after what they'd just been through, she didn't know. But maybe that's how he—and Andre—handled this kind of situation. She'd been married to a cop, knew the dangers that even a routine traffic stop could carry. And Andre was in an even more dangerous position, one that sent him into the line of fire when other law enforcement wasn't enough. How was she going to deal with that?

The thought made her freeze. When had she started thinking of Andre as someone she had a future with? She'd known him forty-eight hours, and part of that time she'd spent under fire or holding him hostage. Even if they knew each other well enough for her thoughts not to be flat-out ridiculous, it could never work.

Not unless she finally got free of Dylan and her past, a voice in her head whispered. The sudden, fierce hope she felt, the wish for a real future instead of what she'd been doing for the past three years, surprised her with its intensity.

"Andre?" she spoke into the phone, and her voice came out small and scared.

"It's okay," he told her. "I'm here. I'm coming."

She coughed, tried to sound strong, because she wasn't scared due to what had just happened with the shooter—or at least, that's not what was scaring her right now. It was the realization of how strong her feelings were for this man. But she couldn't exactly tell him that, not now. Not until she was no longer on the run.

Instead she cleared her throat again and said, "I'm fine. I'm sorry I ran out on you."

Scott was staring, listening to every word, so she turned her back on him for the illusion of privacy and continued, "I was trying to keep you out of trouble. You and your brothers. I didn't realize…I didn't want to—"

Suddenly, strong hands landed on her shoulders and spun her around and then Andre was there in front of her, and she was crushed in his arms. Over her head, she heard him say something to Scott, but his hold on her was so tight, her ears pressed against him, so she couldn't make it out.

Then he held her at arm's length, studying her intently, clearly searching for injuries. She started to tell him she was fine, but he'd already dropped to his knees and was checking her leg for himself.

"Scott's right. It's not serious. But we'll need to get you patched up."

Something else Scott had said came back to her, and she looked at him. "You said the shooter had been up there awhile?"

"Yeah, well, he set up a hide. The agents said it appears to be well used. He's been waiting for you."

Juliette returned her attention to Andre. "Dylan has been in Pennsylvania. So this definitely wasn't him. What about Jim? Has he been off work? Do you think he's been here since those men came into my office?" She couldn't bring herself to say *since the attempted hit on me.*

"I don't know, but we're going to find out."

He held up his hands as a pair of agents came running their way. "She's with me. I need to take her to the hospital, and then we'll go to the WFO. We've got information on the hostage situation from earlier this week."

The agents nodded, and although they didn't look happy, no one tried to slap handcuffs on her again.

Andre took her hand. "Let's go."

"Are you sure? Should I stay—"

"We're getting you stitched up and then it's time to lay everything out in the open for the case agents. It's time to end this."

"A COP FRIEND just paid Keane a visit in Leming," Andre announced three hours later. He was sitting at a conference table at the Washington Field Office with Juliette and a pair of agents. The agents seemed less than impressed by their sudden involvement, not to mention their story about why they hadn't come forward earlier.

If OPR didn't already have his name on a short

list, Andre was sure these agents were going to insist it was added. He'd never met either of them, but they were both veteran agents who'd been wearing frowns since he and Juliette had arrived.

"So, Keane is still in Pennsylvania?" asked the older agent, a man with a thick head of entirely gray hair and a roadmap of lines on his face. He'd introduced himself as Special Agent Porter and apparently expected even Andre to address him by his title.

"He's still there."

"Well, cross him off the list, then," the other agent said. Special Agent Franks was about five years younger than his partner and only slightly more likeable, with intense green eyes that held a little bit of sympathy mixed in with the annoyance.

"For the Quantico shooting anyway," Andre agreed. "Not necessarily for the hit."

"Don't you think it was the same person?" Porter argued.

"Yeah, probably," Andre said, "but not definite." He angled a glance at Juliette, who'd stayed mostly silent after she'd told them her story, putting a lot of emphasis on how Andre wasn't to blame for her actions. Neither of them had mentioned his brothers. Andre wanted to keep them out of it.

"What about Jim?" Juliette spoke up. "Do we know if he's still working? That should be easy to check, right?" She looked at him rather than the agents on the case.

"We're checking that now," Porter answered her. "And while you two were getting coffee, I put in a call to the profiler we had review the hostage situation. She's on her way now."

"I think her theory was right," Franks said, which just made Porter frown more.

"What was her theory?" Andre asked.

"You can ask her yourself," Porter said, staring at a text on his phone. "She's here. Be right back." He stood and left the conference room.

"Don't worry about him," Franks said when he was gone. "He's always in a bad mood."

Andre tried not to let his amusement show; Franks wasn't exactly a ball of fun himself. But any humor quickly faded as he thought about his own future with the Bureau. He knew he was going to be in trouble—the question was how much. He just hoped he hadn't destroyed his career.

But even if he could, he wasn't sure he'd go back and do anything differently, except perhaps not let Juliette out of his sight. He would have preferred they'd gone in together instead of her showing up at Quantico and ending up back under fire.

The door opened again, ending Andre's musing as Porter led in a woman wearing a well-tailored pantsuit. Her hair was up in a tight bun, her pretty features muted by her serious expression. When Andre stood, he towered over her, even though he was only five-ten.

"I'm Evelyn Baine," she introduced herself, shaking his hand and then Juliette's. "I provided a profile on the hostage case yesterday, but the new details Agent Porter just shared give me a lot more insight." She smiled, and he could see she loved her job. "This will help."

"So, what was in your profile?" Andre asked, curious about what Porter had meant earlier.

She propped her hands on her hips, not bothering to sit as Porter settled back into his own seat. "Well, the fact that someone hired ex-cons for the job, and that the *intent* was for them to grab her…" She paused, looking at Juliette apologetically. "Grab you…and kill you without anyone knowing why you'd disappeared suggests a professional, not a personal grudge."

Beside him, Juliette sat a little straighter. "I'd been thinking it was my ex-husband, and I guess we've just determined he wasn't involved in the shooting at Quantico, but we weren't sure about what happened at my office. So, they were both probably planned by Dylan's partner."

Evelyn's lips twisted. "How well did you know his partner?"

Juliette shrugged. "Pretty well. He was Dylan's best man at our wedding. He was over for dinner all the time."

"Tell me about your relationship."

"It was okay, I guess." She glanced at Andre and Evelyn's keen gaze followed, as though she could read their entire history together in that one look. "I was telling Andre that I think Jim was sort of jealous of the time I took from him. Before Dylan and I married, he and Jim did everything together."

Evelyn nodded, and it was clearly what she'd been expecting. "It could have been the partner who did this. We definitely can't rule him out. He's a cop, and so he knows the more distance he has from a murder the less likely he is to be tied to it forensically. But everything about this attempt screams that there was no personal connection."

"Murder is pretty personal," Porter argued.

"Yeah, but if you've secretly—or not so secretly—envied someone for years, where's the payoff? Juliette ran three years ago. She was no longer competition for Dylan's attention. And with a grudge big enough to kill over, most people want to do it personally. But time and distance will dull that kind of grudge."

"Our theory is that Dylan Keane and Jim Valance were helping cover up who really killed Kurt Manning," Andre said. "Juliette overheard Keane take a payoff. We think the hit was an attempt to silence Juliette."

"I agree," Evelyn said. "But I don't think it's either of them who put out the hit. I think you're searching for a third player."

Chapter Eleven

"Well, Jim Valance is missing," Franks announced, taking his attention off the tablet he'd been typing away on for the past ten minutes.

"What do you mean, missing?" Juliette asked, noticing that neither Andre nor the profiler seemed surprised.

She studied Evelyn, taking in her unusual mix of features—the sea green eyes and light brown skin—and the woman's small stature. It was interesting how someone so tiny compared to the three men in the room could project all that confidence. Especially after essentially being told that the theory she'd just announced could be wrong.

"It's got to be Valance we're after, not some mystery third participant," Porter said.

Franks shot him a look that Juliette couldn't quite interpret, then he said, "Valance's chief says he took a day off earlier this week, and he hasn't returned. He was supposed to be in yesterday, but he wasn't. They've checked his house, and there's no sign of him. No sign of a struggle either, and his car is gone."

"So there's a good chance he's nearby," Porter concluded. "Do you know if he's skilled with a rifle?"

"The shooting at Quantico wasn't skilled," Andre said, and Juliette gaped.

"No one was shot," Andre said quietly. "Given the distance and the angles, if he knew what he was doing, he should have been able to hit you."

"He got close," Porter said, eyeing her leg, which was wrapped after she'd gotten the bits of concrete removed.

"Yeah, but if he already put a hit on her, why shoot to scare?" Franks agreed. He asked Juliette, "Is Jim Valance a good shot with a rifle?"

Juliette shrugged. "He's a cop, so I assume so." Dylan had been good with one, which was why she'd recognized the sound. Early in their relationship, when he'd take her shooting, he'd usually let her use a pistol only, but he'd shoot a variety of weapons, and she'd learned to distinguish the sounds.

"That doesn't really mean anything."

When Porter didn't elaborate, Andre explained, "A police officer would be issued a pistol and probably a shotgun as a backup weapon.

But most of them don't shoot rifles on the job, not unless they're in a specialty unit. Being proficient with a pistol doesn't necessarily mean you'd be good with a rifle. The distance is totally different, and he'd have to know how to use a scope properly."

That was what Andre did, Juliette knew. Scott had told her he was one of HRT's best snipers.

"Just because Valance isn't at work doesn't mean he's here," Evelyn spoke up. "Keane left work, too, and he's at a cabin in Pennsylvania. Almost as if he's hiding out."

"Right." Andre spoke up. "We thought he might be hiding from Valance, making it harder for his partner to stage an 'accident' on the job."

"Or someone is after both of them," Evelyn suggested. "What about the person you already suspect has gotten away with murder?"

"Harkin." Andre nodded slowly. "I hadn't considered him."

"Why would he be trying to kill me now?" Juliette asked. "It's been three years. And it's Dylan who's been chasing me all over the country all that time."

"He kept finding you, right?" Evelyn asked.

"Yeah." Juliette bit her lip, considering how long she'd been here feeling safe. Had that just been an illusion from the beginning? "But except for that one time, I always spotted him and ran before he caught up to me. I didn't see him here."

"But maybe he'd found your location and was biding his time. Or he'd narrowed it down to this area but didn't know exactly where. It's possible someone was tracking Keane while he tracked you," Evelyn said.

"Yeah, we thought maybe Jim was," Juliette replied.

"But why *now*?" Evelyn asked.

"Well, that's what I was wondering about Harkin. As far as I'm aware, he never even knew I'd overheard him and Dylan talking. And if he did know all along, why wait three years?"

"That's the key," Evelyn told them, wearing an expression Juliette figured she saved for doing big reveals when she gave profiles. "Determine what the trigger was recently and that will tell you who."

Porter was animated for the first time since Juliette had met him. "You're right. The one thing we know for sure is that Dylan Keane wasn't involved in today's shooting. So, either he's been searching for you all this time and someone else has been helping him, or someone's been following him. And the other person had something happen recently that means you have to go."

"Like what?" Juliette asked, perplexed. She understood Dylan's persistence chasing her until he caught up to her. But why, after all this time, would someone else come after her?

"Someone is threatening to tell," Andre said, and all the other agents in the room nodded. The energy in the room seemed to go up with the feeling that they were onto something. "And one of them decided he needed to eliminate all the loose ends."

She was a loose end.

Juliette didn't say the words out loud, but it was almost as if Andre heard her, because he took her hand under the conference center table and squeezed.

"Jim was always a big spender," she realized. "Your br—uh, you said Dylan was living above his means recently. Jim *always* did. Or at least it seemed that way. He always had the newest electronics, and he was constantly taking these women he met at the clubs to expensive dinners. Maybe the money ran out."

"Maybe he demanded more from Harkin to keep his mouth shut," Evelyn agreed, not commenting on Juliette's slipup, although Juliette was pretty sure she'd noticed.

"That's risky," Franks said. "If he was the one who altered evidence, he was in pretty deep himself."

"Yeah, but he was investigating the case. He

could always say he pulled the file for some reason, noticed something new. I doubt he'd actually do it, given his involvement, but to a murderer who'd gotten away with it, that could be a convincing threat," Andre agreed with Evelyn.

"Can you get Valance's financials?" Evelyn asked the case agents. "That could be the stressor that set off this attempted hit."

"Probably not with what we've got now," Porter said. "But if Valance is having real financial problems, we might see evidence of that even without a warrant. But honestly, the prints on the shell casings at Quantico will probably tell us more."

"What about the convicts we arrested?" Andre spoke up. "They both thought a cop paid them off."

There was silence in the room for a minute, then Juliette said tentatively, "Maybe Harkin was trying to cover his tracks? He's pretty intelligent. He and Manning started that company together. Manning was in charge, but a lot of people in our town seemed to think Harkin was really the brains of it."

Andre nodded. "It's a definite possibility."

"We'll investigate his whereabouts, too," Porter promised, then stood. "Unless there's more you can give us, we need to get back to work."

"Are you going to bring Dylan Keane in?" Andre asked.

"Not yet," Porter said. "Right now, he needs to feel as if no one is onto him. The police department in Leming is keeping eyes on him so he doesn't take off. If we bring him in for questioning now, we're just announcing what we suspect. And we won't be able to hold him, which means he could run. We need something concrete first, then we'll grab him."

Juliette got to her feet slowly, wondering what this meant for her. When she'd shown up at Quantico and tried to explain what had happened, they'd patted her down for weapons and slapped handcuffs on her. It had been humiliating, but she understood it.

"The FBI can offer you a safe house," Franks said.

Juliette looked at Andre, not sure what to do. That might be the most logical thing, but would it mean she'd be trapped in some out-of-the-way house, not involved at all in bringing down whoever had tried to kill her? Even though she wasn't in law enforcement and she knew she couldn't officially investigate, she didn't want to sit on the sidelines. She'd been doing that with her whole life for too long. She wanted to help stop this.

Besides, if she went to a safe house now, would she see Andre again?

"She can stay with me," Andre said, not seeming to care about the smirks from Porter and Franks at his words. "I'll keep her safe."

"WHAT HAVE YOU GOT?" Andre asked, opening the door wide for his brothers and Scott that afternoon. It was beginning to feel like a regular occurrence, all of them gathering to work on Juliette's situation. Although Andre wasn't happy about the circumstances, it was fun to work with his brothers this way. Since all of them worked for different law enforcement agencies, he'd never done that before.

"I've got more pizza," Marcos said.

"I've got beer," Scott contributed.

"And I've got news," Cole finished.

Andre shut the door behind them. "You win," he told Cole. "Let's hear it."

"I've got a little bit of news, too," Marcos said. "I just thought you'd appreciate the food."

"Me, too," Scott said. "But my news isn't case related. Not exactly."

"All right, let's hear all of it," Andre said, ushering them into the living room, where Juliette was waiting, wearing another pair of Shaye's too-long pants and slightly too-tight T-shirts.

When they'd returned from the WFO earlier,

she'd changed out of the clothes she'd worn to Quantico, which had been torn and filthy. Then she'd put her hands on her hips and informed him that she might not have investigative experience, but she knew the players best and she could help. He'd already known he was falling hard for her before that, but watching her stand there so determined had pushed him over the edge.

He stared at her now, looking eager to hear the news his brothers and his partner had brought. She was a natural part of the group, and she seemed at home in his living room. They needed to wrap up this case, because once he could be sure she was out of danger, he was going to ask her to stay in Virginia, to give the two of them a chance at a relationship.

The idea unnerved him, in part because he had no idea if she still considered Pennsylvania home or if she'd want to stay in a place that had just been another city in a long line of hiding places. Not to mention she'd spent most of her time since college either dating, being married to, or running from Dylan Keane. Once she was free of him, would she even want a relationship? Or would she want a chance to be totally independent, completely free of any man?

Pushing the worry aside, Andre sat beside Juliette on the couch as Marcos opened up the pizza on his coffee table.

"Well, since I won," Cole said with a grin as he settled in one of the cushy chairs, "I talked to a detective from Juliette's old town, one cop to another. The case agents had already called a few times today, so they'd gotten the lowdown. Apparently, when Juliette disappeared three years ago, it made the department nervous, since it happened right after they'd ignored her claims." He looked at Juliette. "Keane told them you'd moved back to England to live with your parents."

She sighed. "And they believed that? I didn't spend much time with anyone from the department other than Jim, but I saw them sometimes. *Someone* there should have known I had barely spoken to my parents in years."

"I think they did," Cole replied. "But Keane must have doctored photos, because he produced some of you and your parents, so they bought it. He'd told them you couldn't get over, um, your miscarriage."

"He made that up," Juliette cut in, and Cole seemed relieved.

"Anyway, he said you had to get away for a while and I think they bought it, but a few of them thought the whole thing was odd."

Juliette leaned forward on the couch. "Did anyone check into it?"

"No."

Juliette sat back. She didn't seem surprised

that no one had bothered to see if she'd really left of her own accord or if something had happened to her.

"What kind of slipshod department is this?" Andre demanded.

"Keane was one of their top detectives," Cole reminded him. "And Juliette had never made any complaints before. By the time she did, he'd laid the groundwork for them to dismiss it. I agree that they should have checked it out, but it's not really surprising they didn't. You always want to give your colleague—especially one who's probably saved your life a time or two—the benefit of the doubt."

Andre nodded grudgingly. HRT was a brotherhood, which was something he loved about it. A good police department would be the same way. If one of his HRT buddies had been accused of something like this, he probably wouldn't have believed it either. Everyone had blind spots.

The thought took him back to his dream from that morning. "Hey, this is unrelated, but later we need to talk." He looked at Cole, sitting on his big chair, and Marcos, perched on the armrest. "It's about the fire." He didn't need to explain which one.

They both seemed quizzical, but nodded.

"So, anyway," Cole continued, "since the FBI has been asking for information, one of the officers pulled the Manning case and went over it again, and I asked him if I could review the forensic evidence."

"And?"

"And Loews's fingerprint was found at the scene. It was on a pen that was under the body. The theory at the time was that either any prints were wiped down and this one got missed because of its location, or more likely that Loews actually had the pen on him and didn't realize he'd dropped it."

"So, basically, it would be easy for someone else to drop," Marcos said.

"Yeah, but not one of the detectives. The responding officer found the pen. It was fingerprinted at the scene. So, if it was left behind, then the killer did it."

"Well, actually that makes sense," Andre said. "If we're going with the theory that Loews and Harkin were working together and Harkin paid off the detectives. Juliette heard Harkin tell her ex that he'd keep him out of it but couldn't help Loews. That's probably why. Loews dropped the pen at the scene and didn't realize it and it was too late for the detectives to make that evidence go away."

"The detective I spoke to *did* say that he remembered Keane being gung ho on Harkin being the killer, *not* Loews, until one day he jumped in with his partner saying it was Loews. They were surprised, because he'd been insisting so loudly for so long, but they figured the evidence didn't bear it out."

"Any word on Jim Valance's whereabouts?" Andre asked.

"Nope. They're searching for him, but haven't found anything. They've had a bulletin out on his license plate since he didn't show up for work, because they were worried something bad could have happened to him, but there have been no hits on it yet."

Andre looked up at his younger brother, who was already on his third slice of pizza. "What did you dig up?"

"I talked to Kendry again ten minutes before I got here. He checked earlier today and Keane was still at the cabin. But given everything that's happening, I suspect Keane's department is going to call him home soon. And Kendry promises to check again in the morning."

"Scott?" Andre asked.

"Well, not to add any more pressure to this situation, but I need Nadia's weapon. I promised her I'd bring it back to Quantico tomorrow."

Juliette flushed. "Will you tell her I'm sorry? I left the bullets in the trash can outside the bathroom."

"Yeah, we found those," Scott said. "And I

will. But you should probably tell her yourself when this is all over, because otherwise, the next time she sees you, she might use her persuasive techniques to get a personal apology. And by persuasive techniques, I mean her notorious chokehold."

He said it as though it was a given Juliette would be sticking around, and Andre wanted his partner to be right, but from the surprise on Juliette's face, he wasn't sure.

"I also talked to someone at OPR," Scott continued. "Unofficially. He can't promise me anything, and he only talked to me at all because my sister saved his life a few years ago." Scott turned to Juliette and explained, "My sister is a SWAT agent." He returned his attention to Andre. "Anyway, he says if the investigation shows a reasonable belief on Juliette's part that she couldn't trust law enforcement to help her and *if* you weren't unreasonably hindering an investigation, it'll just be a mark in your file. He says you might get off with a verbal warning, but he doubts it."

"Who decides this?" Juliette asked, nerves clear in her voice. "What can I do to prove to them that this is my fault and not Andre's?"

"Don't worry," Andre told her, relieved that the agent didn't think he would be suspended—

or worse. He was surprised, because part of him was expecting it.

"Well, I am wor—" she started, but the ringing of Andre's and Cole's phones at the same time cut her off.

"That's weird," Andre said as they both answered, and then he looked over at Cole, wondering if his brother was getting the same news he was right now. From the expression on Cole's face, he was.

"What is it?" Marcos asked as they both hung up.

"They just found Jim Valance. He's dead."

Chapter Twelve

"What?" Juliette gaped at him. "Jim is dead? How?"

"A homeless man stumbled across his body in an old warehouse. The place was condemned, so no one was supposed to be in there," Cole said.

Juliette nodded. She knew exactly which warehouse he was talking about. Everyone in town knew it. The warehouse had been condemned for as long as she could remember, but somehow it never got bulldozed, and every few years, police had to rouse squatters from it. "It's a good place to hide a body. Usually, no one goes in there until it *really* starts getting cold outside, generally December."

"Well, estimated time of death is yesterday afternoon," Andre contributed, his expression hard to read.

"Right before Dylan left town," Juliette said. It made sense, in a way. If Jim was trying to go after Harkin for more money, he was probably putting pressure on Dylan to help, too. She should have realized earlier that Dylan wouldn't have been in this alone—he and Jim always worked as a team. If Jim pushed hard enough and Dylan wanted to put it all behind him, maybe he'd snapped.

But somehow, even though the idea of Dylan trying to kill her didn't seem far-fetched, she couldn't imagine him turning on Jim.

She shook her head. "You talked about the law enforcement brotherhood? Dylan and Jim were like brothers." It was a connection that had always seemed to go deeper than his loyalty to her. The loyalty she knew she'd completely broken when she'd confronted him.

"He chased you pretty determinedly," Andre said.

"Yeah, but you've been putting doubt in my mind that his intent was to kill me. Either way," she rushed on when Andre seemed ready to keep arguing, "he knew Jim a lot longer than me. They weren't just partners. They grew up together."

"Getting back to Valance," Scott said quickly, not giving Andre time to respond, "What happened to him?"

"He was shot in the head with a small-caliber weapon. They should know more in a day or two, after the autopsy. The locals are handling the scene, and so far if they have anything useful forensically, they're not sharing. They do know the gun was unregistered."

She wondered if that was supposed to mean something to her. Of course a cop would know not to use his own weapon, but she assumed most people wouldn't do that if the murder was premeditated.

"Was he moved, or did someone lure him to that warehouse?" Marcos asked.

"He was killed there," Andre said. "So either it was a meeting place no one would see or someone took Valance there under duress and then killed him."

"Doesn't that mean it was probably Harkin?" Juliette asked. "There's no reason for Jim and Dylan not to be seen together. They're partners."

"Well, I was digging up information on Harkin while you were in the shower earlier today," Andre began. Somehow, the words sounded intimate, as though they really shared a home instead of this temporary situation. "And he filed a flight plan for his private plane to fly down to an island off the coast of Florida this week. Supposedly, he left at the beginning of the week, which would give him an alibi."

"Supposedly?" Juliette asked.

"It's his own plane," Cole jumped in. "Right

now, all we know is that he filed a flight plan. There's a chance he could have filed the plan and not actually taken the flight. Or the flight might have happened with someone else on it."

"Whether or not the flight took off should be easy to confirm, but it'll take a little longer, because we're dealing with private airstrips. As for him sending someone in his place?" Andre shrugged. "Unlikely but definitely possible. We'll have to dig a little deeper on that."

Could Dylan really have killed Jim? Juliette wasn't sure why that was so hard for her to imagine, after the horrible things she'd thought Dylan was willing to do to her. But it didn't feel right. Dylan and Jim's friendship not only went way back, but it was also a bond she couldn't imagine him betraying—maybe because unlike her relationship with Dylan, Jim's had been on equal footing, a brotherhood. "I don't think Dylan did this," she insisted, noticing Andre's frown deepen.

There was an awkward silence for a minute, then Marcos broke it. "Well, with a cop dead and his police force investigating, plus the WFO agents on your case, plus all of us, we'll find answers soon." He gave her a wide grin and added, "You've got a heck of a team on your side."

Juliette managed to smile, because it was true. She *did* have a heck of a team. But then her gaze was drawn back to Andre, who was sitting close enough to touch on the couch beside her. All she'd have to do was stretch out her hand a tiny bit and take his. But somehow, he felt far away right now.

Once they had their answers, what would it mean for her and Andre?

THREE HOURS LATER, Andre faced his brothers, who both wore expectant, slightly nervous expressions. Scott had headed home to his fiancée half an hour ago, and Juliette had gone to bed a few minutes ago. She'd claimed she was exhausted from the day, which was probably true, but he suspected her real reason for leaving the room was to give him time alone with Cole and Marcos.

"She's totally crazy about you," Marcos said now, obviously noticing where his attention had strayed.

"Don't mess this up," Cole added, in what Andre and Marcos jokingly called his "big brother" voice.

"This whole thing with her ex…" Andre shook his head.

"One way or another, he's going to end up behind bars. If he's *not* the one who killed Valance and hired the convicts to go after Juliette, there's still the matter of taking a payoff from a murderer." Marcos leaned back in his chair, as though that was all there was to it.

"You're worried she's still hung up on him?" Cole asked. "Because I don't think so."

"Not exactly." Although he had, just a little, when she'd insisted Keane was innocent in his partner's murder. "I guess I'm just worried that once this is all over, she won't really even know what she wants."

Marcos made a face at him. "She's a grown-up."

"Yeah, but she spent her life being sent off to boarding schools by parents who had no interest, then she married this guy, who was obviously a real winner, and then she's spent all these years running from him. I don't want to take advantage of the fact that I might be the first guy who's treated her decently."

Both his brothers were silent, then Marcos said, "She seems pretty self-reliant. She managed to stay ahead of this guy for three years, right?" When Andre nodded, he continued, "She didn't lean on anyone during all of that time. That takes a lot of willpower. Besides, she was willing to turn herself in for you. That's pretty huge."

Andre hadn't really thought about that. He'd spent so much of his energy today worrying about her when he'd woken to find her gone, and then dealing with the aftermath. They hadn't really had a chance to talk about why she'd gone to the FBI herself. But suddenly her words during their phone call at the scene of the shooting came back to him.

I was trying to keep you out of trouble. You and your brothers.

"This might not be what you want to hear," Cole said, "but if this ends, and she's finally free, logic says she won't stay in one of the places she was hiding. Especially not with the way she talked about her job the other day. As if it was a placeholder for what she really wanted to do, but she knew the job she wanted would make it too easy for her ex to track her. If she does stay, then I think you'll have your answer."

Andre nodded. His brothers made sense, but there was still a voice in the back of his head warning him that relationships forged in these kinds of circumstances didn't last. Not that they even had a relationship. He wasn't sure exactly *what* they had, but hour by hour, it *felt* more like a relationship, at least on his end.

And Marcos was right about one thing: the fact that she'd been willing to put herself in danger to keep him and his brothers out of trouble? All of a sudden, he wanted to send his brothers home and kiss her for that. Preferably for a very long time.

"So, what was this about the fire?" Marcos asked when Andre went silent.

He shook himself out of thoughts about Juliette, on the other side of the wall, probably tucked into bed in the nightgown Shaye had lent her. "Did either of you ever read the report on it?"

They both sat a little straighter and nodded, and Andre knew his surprise showed. None of them had ever talked about it. But then again, they were similar in so many ways. Probably the same thing that had driven them all into law enforcement had driven them to need answers.

"It was an accident," Cole said. "The fire started at the back of the house. Someone left some candles lit after going to bed. They were close to papers on the desk, and it spread fast from there."

"Stupid," Marcos hissed, and the frustration in his voice took Andre back to those terrifying moments watching Cole tamp out the fire on his younger brother, of the hours at the hospital while their burns were treated.

Cole's had been superficial, mostly to his hands. Over the years, the scars had faded until they were no longer visible at all. Marcos would carry a reminder of the fire on his back for the rest of his life.

"I don't think it was an accident," Andre told them.

Cole leaned forward. "Why?"

"Everyone was supposed to be upstairs, asleep, at the time of the fire, right?"

His brothers nodded.

"But I don't think everyone was. I've been dreaming about that night ever since that call I got a few days ago."

"To the scene where the father set the house on fire with his wife and kid inside," Marcos said.

Surprise made Andre sit back, and Cole added, "Scott told us about it. He thought it might bring back memories."

"You didn't say anything."

"Yeah, well, you got pretty busy right afterward," Cole said, tipping his head in the direction Juliette had disappeared.

"Who wasn't sleeping at the time of the fire?" Marcos asked, bringing them back on topic.

"Our foster father," Andre said. "And one of the other kids." He racked his mind for the name of the girl who'd joined them in the house a few months before the fire started. "Brenna."

"No way," Marcos said instantly, reminding Andre that Brenna had only been a year younger than Marcos then—putting her around eleven—and that Marcos had developed his first crush the day she arrived.

"What makes you think they weren't sleeping when the fire started?" Cole asked, lines furrowing his forehead.

"They were coming from around the back of the house. Everyone else was in the front or coming out the side door, logical if they'd come from upstairs."

"Maybe they came out the front, then went around to the back to see if there was another way to get the rest of us out," Marcos suggested.

"Maybe," Andre agreed. "I guess that could make sense if it was just him. But why would he take Brenna with him?"

"She followed him?" Cole suggested.

"I don't know." Andre shook his head. "The dreams I've been having have been bothering me, as though I was forgetting something important. And then when I remembered where they'd been, it all clicked into place."

Being with Juliette had helped it click, Andre realized now. As they'd worked to unravel who was coming after her, they'd put doubts in her mind about her past—both that it was Keane after her, and that what she'd overheard really meant what she thought it did.

His own past was suddenly the same way—a

nebulous thing, instead of set in stone the way he'd always accepted.

"Why would either of them set fire to the house?" Cole asked, always the reasonable one, bringing Andre's mind back to the conversation. "Our foster dad lost his house that day. It wasn't salvageable at all. And Brenna had only been there a few months. What reason would she have to set a fire?"

"Do you think someone was hurting her, and we didn't know it?" Marcos asked.

They all knew it could happen. All three of them had been in multiple foster homes over the years, and all of them had seen both good and bad. And they'd lost track of Brenna after that day, so whatever secrets she had, she'd taken with her.

"She never said anything," Cole said slowly. "And if she set the fire, he didn't turn her in. Which suggests either that she wasn't to blame or that he had something bigger to cover up."

When Marcos's face darkened, Andre said, "There were a lot of kids through that house. It wasn't exactly full of love and sunshine, but I never saw or heard anything terrible or suspicious."

"I didn't either," Cole agreed.

"So then why?" Marcos asked.

"There could be a perfectly logical explanation," Cole stressed, but as Andre knew they were all thinking the same thing.

The fire that day had split them apart, sent each of them off into new foster homes on their own, with no one to have their backs. It had been a defining moment in all of their lives. Having brothers ripped from them after they'd finally found a new family had impacted each of them hugely. If someone had caused it, no matter the reason, Andre wanted to know why.

Once they helped Juliette get out of danger, it was time to dig into their past.

DREAD ABOUT WHAT he might find in his past and worry about what his future could hold consumed Andre as he stood in the doorway to the guest room. But as Juliette stirred under the covers, opening her eyes and staring back at him, the present seemed very clear.

She blinked a few times and sat up. The covers fell to her waist and he noticed she was wearing his FBI shirt instead of the nightgown Shaye had sent.

A wave of possessiveness swept through him.

"What's wrong?" she asked, her voice heavy with sleep.

"Nothing." He didn't move, just stayed rooted in the doorway, watching her and wondering if he should have waited until morning for this.

She held out her hand. "Did you talk to your brothers about the fire?"

It was all the encouragement he needed. Pushing away from the door frame, he went and sat on the edge of the bed, taking the hand she offered in both of his. "Yeah, I did. We're going to worry about it later."

"You want to tell me about it?"

He shrugged. It wasn't why he'd come into her room, but he found he *did* want to talk to her about it. "The house that Cole, Marcos and I lived in burned down when I was fourteen. We always thought it was an accident, but now I'm not so sure."

She swore softly and he had to laugh, because with everything that had happened over the past few days, it was the first time he'd heard her swear.

"That day was really scary," he said, stroking the soft skin on her hand. "But the real tragedy for us was that it split us up. The foster parents we lived with then lost their house and so all the kids went different places. When I moved into that house, it felt like home for the first time since my parents died. Not really because of the foster parents, but Cole. He treated me as if I was his real brother, from day one. And then Marcos came into the house, and it was the same thing. It was this instant connection, as though we shared a blood bond."

Juliette smiled and in the darkness, her eyes had a stormy quality, because he couldn't see the flecks of blue amidst the hazel. "I can see it. The three of you even look alike."

He must have seemed skeptical, because she laughed and added, "Not physically. But there's something about the expressions you make, this intense thing all three of you get. When it happens at the same time, it's obvious you're brothers."

No one had ever told him that before, and the idea made him smile. "Did you know that when Cole got out of foster care, he took on multiple jobs so he could get a place and take me and Marcos in when we hit eighteen?"

"Wow," she said softly. "That's a pretty amazing family you have."

It was, and it made him think of how she'd grown up—with blood relatives who'd left her to tackle life on her own. He twined their hands together more tightly. "What about you? Any family you're close to?"

She shrugged. "My grandma and I were really close when I was young, before she died. It's why I picked her last name to use here, because she showed me what family was supposed to be. But otherwise? Not really. I had some cousins in England I got along with well, but my parents sent me to the US when I hit middle school, so I only saw them once every few years after that."

"You didn't go home for holidays?"

"Not usually."

The sadness he was feeling for her must have shown, because she said, "It was hard at first, but I made friends. In college, too. Honestly, part of my loneliness was my own fault. I've never been good at letting people get too close. I always worry they'll disappear." She flushed, as though the admission embarrassed her.

"I'm not going to disappear." The words came out of his mouth before he'd really thought them through, but they must have been the right ones, because she leaned forward and kissed him.

Unlike the kisses they'd shared before, this one was tender and brief, like a couple who'd known each other a long time. It was less about desire and more about comfort and connection, but as he slid his hand through the silky strands of her hair that fell forward when she kissed him, he wanted more.

She must have felt the same thing, because she slid out from underneath the covers and scooted closer, not breaking contact. Then her arms were around his neck and she was stroking his tongue with hers as his hands found the bare softness of her legs.

"Mmm," she mumbled softly, sliding even closer to him and making his T-shirt ride up her thighs.

She kept kissing him—slow, deep kisses that were making him crazy as he avoided her bandage and skimmed his hands up and down her legs. "This isn't why I came in here," he said semicoherently.

Pulling back slightly, Juliette gave him a seductive smile. "Really? Why'd you come in here?"

"I wanted to talk about the future." He was jumping the gun and he knew it. But despite the fact that he could spend hours on a rifle scope totally still and silent, when it came to his personal life, he wasn't good at waiting. When he wanted something, he dove in headfirst.

She looked wary as she asked, "What about it?"

"When this is all over, and we've got your ex and whoever else is involved behind bars, I'm hoping you'll stay in Virginia."

Surprise flitted across her face, and he wondered if this was a mistake, if he should have just kept pursuing her until she gave him a real chance, rather than giving her time to think too much about it. But since it was already out there, he kept pushing. "I want us to get to know each other under more normal circumstances. I want to take you out on real dates, kiss you good-night on your porch."

She hesitated, and he knew that whatever feelings she had for him, on some level she wasn't ready for another serious relationship.

"It's okay," he said before she could shoot him down. "You don't have to answer right now. Just think about it."

"Right now, I need to—" Juliette started, but whatever she was going to say was cut off by the ringing of his phone.

He scowled at it, not just because of the bad timing, but also because it was late. The read-out said Cole.

Cursing, he picked up. "What's happening?"

"Uh, did I wake you?" Cole asked. "I thought you'd still be up, since we didn't leave all that long ago."

"No, I'm up," Andre said, staring at Juliette, who was tugging the shirt back down her legs.

"Shaye's been up late, reviewing the forensic details from the Manning murder."

"What does she think?"

"Well, you're not going to like this, but she thinks this is more than just a couple of cops helping one murderer stay out of jail. She thinks Loews was framed. Shaye thinks he's actually innocent."

Chapter Thirteen

What was wrong with her?

Juliette mentally cursed herself for her idiocy. Andre had offered her a chance at exactly what she'd wanted—him—and she'd frozen. Worse, she knew she was right not to make any promises now.

Even if they brought down her ex, even if she was safe for the first time in years, was she really ready to be in a relationship again? The idea of being with Andre was exciting, but it was also terrifying.

When she'd married Dylan, she'd thought that was it. She'd found her forever. She hadn't had any doubts when she'd said yes to his proposal, hadn't suspected they'd be anything but happy together. The end had come out of nowhere, even if in retrospect she could see that the relationship hadn't been right.

Andre was a good guy—she didn't doubt that.

But the fear she'd shared with him earlier hadn't gone away: How did she know she could trust her own judgment about what was right for her? About *who* was right for her? And was she even in the kind of place where she should be in a relationship at all?

Yet, the thought of throwing away a chance to be with Andre made her feel physically ill.

"How is that possible?" Andre was asking into the phone, bringing her attention back to the present.

Finally, he hung up the phone with his brother so she could ask, "What did he say?"

"What were *you* going to say?" Andre asked, setting his phone on the bed and taking her hand again. There was nervousness in the depths of his gaze, and he always seemed so sure of himself that the expression didn't seem right on him.

Her breath came faster. Could she tell him she was scared? That even though she had feelings for him, she wasn't sure she was ready to act on them? It wouldn't be fair to ask him to wait around until she was ready, but maybe they could put this on hold, just for now.

"Can we wait to talk about you and me until after this is over? I need to be able to put this all behind me before I can think about moving forward." It felt like a cop-out, but it was the truth, too. Maybe once Dylan was really, truly out of her life, she'd feel more confident about any decisions she made.

Disappointment flashed across his face, but then he hid it and pressed a quick kiss to her lips. "I get it." He didn't give her a chance to elaborate, and his tone shifted into what she'd come to recognize as his serious work voice. "Cole just heard from Shaye. She studied the forensic details from the case file, and she thinks Loews is innocent."

"What?" Juliette gaped at him. "But the pen was found *under* the body. It had his prints. You think Harkin framed him," she realized. "But what about what I heard Dylan saying to Harkin, about not being able to keep Loews out of it?"

"Are you sure that's exactly what you heard him say? Is there any chance you misunderstood?"

She thought back to that moment three years ago that had changed her life. She'd walked into the house from the side door, and she hadn't taken her car that day, so Dylan hadn't heard her. She hadn't realized he was there, either, because both of them had planned to be out all day. But when she'd walked toward the stairs, she'd heard voices from the kitchen. She'd stopped as soon as she'd heard the unfamiliar voice with Dylan.

She remembered the exact instant she'd recognized it from news footage as Harkin's voice.

She remembered her disbelief, then the anger, then the panic.

Could she really be one hundred percent positive of Dylan's exact words from that day? Some parts of it seemed stamped in her memory, but other parts felt hazy, as if they were a dream. Still… "I think so. If it wasn't exact, it was close."

"So, Keane told Harkin, 'I'll keep you out of it, but there's nothing I can do for Loews now'?"

"Yeah."

"Hmm."

"Why does Shaye think the pen was planted?"

"She says that Loews's print was the only one on the pen."

"So?"

"So, it was a perfect print, easy to pull, and yet there was nothing else. No smudges, nothing."

"That sounds a little odd," Juliette agreed. "But maybe the fact that Manning landed on the pen smudged off the other prints? Besides, shouldn't the original forensics expert have noticed that if it were a problem? Or Loews's experts at the trial?"

"Probably," Andre said. "But either it didn't come up, or it didn't sway anyone. But I find it strange. It's not weird to find no useable prints or to find partials from multiple people or just smudges, but to get one print that's exactly what you need and nothing else should have made someone's alarms go off. It sounds way too convenient to me. If I'd been the investigator, I'd have been suspicious."

"So, this is about more than putting away a murderer," Juliette summed up, feeling herself go pale. "If Shaye is right, then by running when I did, I basically helped Dylan put an innocent man in jail."

WE'RE NOT GOING to know for sure if Loews is innocent until we find Harkin. We need to figure out if he's really in Florida," Andre said, but he could tell by Juliette's stricken expression that she was only half listening.

"It sounded as if Loews and Harkin were in it together, that they were both guilty," she said, her voice baffled and horrified.

"They might have been," Andre said, trying to focus on their conversation instead of their proximity on the bed. "Right now, this is just Shaye's theory."

She gave a smile that didn't reach her eyes. "Cole said Shaye was the best."

"She's pretty good, but my brother has had a crush on Shaye for a couple of years now, so he's easily swayed by her opinion."

"Or part of *why* he's into her is because she's

so good at what she does," Juliette said, and Andre knew it was true.

"Let's just try not to get ahead of ourselves here." He knew exactly what she was doing right now, blaming herself for one more thing that wasn't her fault. "You can't make yourself feel responsible for other people's bad deeds."

"If I'd known—if I'd even *suspected*—I never would have—"

"You tried to turn in your husband, and the police ignored you," Andre reminded her. "That took guts."

"Yeah, but I would have kept trying if I'd thought an innocent man was paying for Harkin's crime." Her forehead furrowed, as though she was trying to figure out how she would have done that and stayed ahead of a husband who'd threatened to kill her if she told.

"But you didn't know," Andre said. "So all we can do now is figure out the truth and make sure whoever should pay goes to jail."

A tremor ran through her, so subtle he wouldn't have noticed it if he hadn't taken her hand earlier. Was it the thought of her husband— a cop—landing in jail? They had protocols for that, separation plans, because cops didn't tend to fare well in prison.

He remembered what she'd asked earlier— she'd wondered if Keane might have taken the payoff because Harkin had threatened Juliette. Although he didn't feel any sympathy for the man who'd violated his professional duty and taken money to let a murderer go free, Andre's animosity lessened just a little at the idea that Keane might have been at all motivated by the desire to keep Juliette safe.

"Once we find out the extent of Keane's involvement, if we can get him to cooperate in bringing down Harkin, I'll try to do what I can for him," Andre said. He didn't add that the promise would be void if it turned out Keane *had* been the one trying to kill Juliette. If that were the case, Andre was going to be sure he spent the rest of his miserable life behind bars.

Surprise flashed across Juliette's face, and then she shifted on the bed to face him. "It probably seems—" she frowned, clearly searching for the right words, then continued "—strange that I would care at all what happens to Dylan."

"Not at—"

She cut him off. "I don't love him anymore."

The words gave him hope, strong enough he actually felt it in his chest. If she really meant that, if she'd truly put her feelings for her ex behind her, then they did have a chance. And although he had real concerns about her being in a place where she knew what she wanted for herself, he wasn't afraid to wait. Staring at her now, sitting so close to him in his guest bed, her hair slightly wild from either sleep or his hands a few minutes earlier, he knew that when this was over, he was going to fight for her.

"But once, I loved him enough to promise my life to him," Juliette continued, not seeming to realize he'd made a big decision. "Even after all the things he's done—or might have done—there's still a part of me that feels bound by that promise. Not to share my life with him," she amended quickly enough that Andre wondered what expression he'd made. "But if he *wasn't* actually trying to kill me—if it's been Jim or Harkin all this time—then I feel as though I at least owe him something. Maybe just some measure of forgiveness," she finished softly.

He smiled at her, because that was probably more than he'd be willing to offer someone who'd threatened to kill him, regardless of whether the person ever tried to carry out the threat. The thought reminded him of his suspicions about the fire, and he wondered what the goal was if it had been arson. Had the fire just gotten out of control, or had someone wanted to kill one of the people in the house?

His foster father had held a blue-collar job, his foster mother had worked part-time out of the house, and they'd used the money from having foster kids to bridge the gap. He'd never seen either of them do anything that would put them in danger. And everyone else in the house had been kids. Cole had been the oldest, but he was only fifteen at the time.

It didn't make sense. Could he be wrong?

As soon as he thought it, he dismissed the idea. Whether or not the fire had been intentional, he was pretty sure that his foster dad and Brenna had been in the back of the house where the fire started. And that meant there was a story no one knew. When Juliette was safe, he was determined to figure out what it was, and he knew Cole and Marcos felt the same way.

"You think that's silly?" Juliette asked, and Andre realized he'd gone silent for too long.

"No. I think it takes a special kind of strength to give that kind of forgiveness."

She smiled up at him, her expression soft and almost shy, and he got to his feet before he did something she'd already said she wasn't ready for, like pull her to him and do his best to never let go.

"In the morning, we'll figure out a plan of action to finish this."

Juliette leaned back against the headboard, her mouth forming a silent *O*. He could tell she was surprised he wasn't staying.

Then she sat forward again, and he knew he needed to get out of there before he broke his promise to give her time to figure out what she wanted. "Good night," he said, then practically ran from the room.

"WE DON'T REALLY know anything until we find Harkin," Andre said softly into his cell phone early the next morning as he nursed a cup of coffee at his kitchen table, alone.

Juliette was still asleep, and although she'd only been in his house a few days, he already missed their easy companionship in the morning, the way her sleepy eyes instantly widened with just one sip of his coffee. If he needed an excuse to keep making it strong, that was it.

"Well, I spoke to the case agents and they're still trying to find him. They're in touch with officials on the island off the coast of Florida where he supposedly flew early this week, but so far, there's no sign of him," Scott said. "They've got a local agent heading over to talk to airline officials at the private airport where his plane landed. They'll try to get a confirmation one way or another."

"If he didn't take that flight, he probably drove here. Did they ever locate Valance's car?"

"I don't think so, but if Harkin has gotten away with killing Loews and a cop, I doubt he'd be dumb enough to take that cop's vehicle."

"True. Do we know what Harkin drives?" Andre asked.

Scott snorted. "A lot. The guy apparently collects cars, both high-end and classic. With Juliette's statement, the case agents got a little leeway in pulling information on Harkin, but that's a lot of cars to try to track down. So far, there's no sign of any of them, but that doesn't mean much. For all we know, he had his secretary rent him a car before he took Harkin's flight to Florida."

"All right. What have you heard about the shell casings used at Quantico?" Andre tried to hide his frustration, but he was sure Scott could hear it. He'd been on HRT for years, so it had been a while since he'd worked a case, but doing it this way—outside the loop—was frustrating. Although HRT required him to sit with his eye pressed to a rifle scope for hours, sometimes days, on end, he'd gotten used to that sort of "hurry up and wait" scenario. This kind of waiting, with the ability to take the next steps with Juliette hanging in the balance, had him on edge.

"Yeah, you're not going to like this. The guy wore gloves to load them. We've got nothing."

"And the hide?"

"It's odd. I went up there myself," Scott said, and Andre was glad, because no one knew hides the way snipers did, because they made hides all the time.

"How so?"

"Well, remember how I said the shooting was obviously someone without a lot of experience on a rifle? The same is true of the hide. It was functional, in a way. He was definitely *trying* to create something to blend into his surroundings, but it was amateurish. I think he got training somewhere, but not professionally."

"You think he took some kind of shoddy civilian training?"

"That would be my guess. It's as though he knew the theory, but not quite how to put it into practice."

"Juliette said Keane knew how to shoot a rifle, and now that we know Valance was dead when the attack at Quantico happened…"

"Harkin is our best suspect," Scott finished. "Yeah, that makes sense. He's got the money to take that kind of training for kicks, and it fits with what I've been seeing in my research. This guy did a lot of weekend training programs— race car driving, skiing, even wine making—but didn't stick with anything. I'll see if I can find anything about firearms training."

"I think our best bet is to locate him now."

"Locate who now?" Juliette asked, yawning

as she walked into the kitchen in his T-shirt and not much else.

He loved that look on her. The thought danced around in his mind, filling him with mild panic. Despite how little time he'd known her, his feelings were too strong, too protective, too intense to be simple attraction. He had no idea when it had begun—probably the moment she'd walked through his door—but he was falling in love with her. Fast.

And she didn't know what she wanted when this was all over. He wasn't even sure she'd committed to staying in Virginia.

"What's the matter?" Juliette asked.

"Nothing. Just getting info from Scott," Andre replied, glad to hear his voice at least sounded normal.

She looked suspicious, but didn't press it as she helped herself to a cup of coffee, topping it off with a generous dose of cream.

"Wimp," he mouthed at her.

Scott continued, "Yeah, the case agents are working on locating Harkin now. But one more thing I *can* tell you about him? The guy owned a lot of guns. And I mean, a *lot*. As though he was a collector. So, whether or not it was him who shot at Quantico yesterday—and I'm thinking it was—he owned more than one rifle."

"Well, that's good. So, even if we don't have

prints, we'll probably be able to match the casings to a rifle when we arrest him," Andre said.

"Yeah. Now we just need to find him."

Chapter Fourteen

"We found him."

"What?" Andre stood in the doorway of his house, staring at Franks and Porter, who'd shown up unannounced, wearing rumpled suits and excited expressions.

Juliette walked up behind him, thankfully having changed out of his T-shirt and into another set of Shaye's borrowed clothes. "You found Harkin?"

The two agents shared a look, and even though they'd known Andre was keeping an eye on Juliette, he could see exactly what they were thinking. He would have been annoyed, except they were right. There was nothing professional about the way he felt about her.

"Where is he?" Not giving them time to answer, Andre said, "If you're planning an arrest, I want in on it." The guy had shot at Juliette. Andre wanted to be there. Ideally, he'd be the one to slap on the handcuffs and let Harkin know he'd be facing a lifetime in prison by the time they were finished with him.

"That's why we're here," Franks said and Andre knew his surprise showed; he'd expected to need to fight to be included.

Andre held open the door. "Come on in."

Franks seemed amused that they'd only been invited in after agreeing to let him help, but Porter's usual serious expression didn't change as Andre led them to his living room. They sat on the two chairs, leaving him and Juliette the couch.

Juliette settled in next to him, at the kind of distance they'd expect if she was a simple witness. Andre longed to take her hand in his and squeeze, but he resisted and stared at the case agents instead, waiting for more details.

"Harkin may have killed Valance, who was a veteran police officer. Whatever the circumstances, we're considering Harkin a high threat. Normally, we'd bring in our SWAT team, but given your involvement—" Porter's gaze went to Juliette again as he finished "—we thought you'd be interested in kicking down the door for us."

"Absolutely," Andre said. Normally, as a sniper, he had high ground, meaning it was his responsibility to survey the situation below and to keep his team members safe. But he'd trained as a regular operator too, in all kinds of dangerous setups. Kicking down a door to get to one armed multimillionaire should be simple.

"Good," Franks said. "It's a little atypical and we had to get special permission, but you've assisted the investigation and you have insight into the players that could be useful." Unsaid but hanging in the air was that he'd helped only after he'd hindered it by hiding Juliette.

"What about Dylan?" Juliette asked. "Are you going to bring him in now, too? We know he left town after his partner's murder. Even if he didn't kill Jim, he's still involved in this whole thing somehow."

"No," Porter said.

Franks explained, "Valance's murder is technically a local investigation. We're coordinating with them because of a possible connection, but right now, there's no evidence Keane killed him. We're after Harkin for the Quantico shooting— that's *our* jurisdiction."

"We can bring Keane in, lean on him and try to get him to break," Porter told Juliette. "But your ex is a cop. Not only will he have a union rep and a lawyer, he knows the drill. He'll figure out pretty quickly we don't have anything and then he'll know we're onto him."

"We're hoping Harkin will give us the leverage we need to hold Keane," Franks added. "Because we *do* have more on Harkin. It's not a slam dunk by any means."

"I used up a favor with a judge for this one," Porter grumbled.

Franks rolled his eyes. "But we found a record of a special firearms training course he took last year. I showed his instructor the hide outside of Quantico and she swears that's his work. It won't hold for long, but it'll get us an arrest and a chance to test fire Harkin's rifle. Hopefully our labs can connect the rifle to the shooting and then if he's smart, he'll be begging to help us."

Porter leaned forward, looking antsy. "Let's get moving. Diaz, call your partner and see if he wants in. Then we'll handle the paperwork and get moving. We got a hit on one of Harkin's cars early this morning and an unmarked police car followed it to a residential location. The police are keeping a discreet eye on it, making sure we know if he moves, but this is a good spot to take him down. It's out of the way, so there won't be any collateral nearby."

"It turns out to be the home of one of Harkin's employees, a woman he apparently sees socially on and off. Anyway, she's in Europe, finishing a deal for him, so he knew she wouldn't be there. We talked to her today and confirmed that Harkin has the code to the house. She had no idea he was there."

"You made sure she knew she'd be in legal trouble if she gave him the heads up, right?" Andre asked.

"We did, but that won't be a problem." Porter laughed and it sounded strangely forced coming from him. "She was pissed."

"She was digging for information on why we were asking about him," Franks added. "And she happened to mention that he's always been a hard-ass to work for, but over the past few years, ever since he took over the company, his corporate tactics have gotten a lot more brutal."

"Did she suspect he had anything to do with Manning's murder?" Juliette spoke up.

"Nah, I don't think so," Porter answered. "But she didn't sound surprised that the FBI was investigating him about something. She probably figures it has to do with his unethical business practices. She was going on and on about not having any choice but to do what he told her to do when it came to deals."

"Our white-collar squad might be investigating that business once we wrap this up," Franks said.

Andre tried not to jump to his feet. He was far less interested in what happened with the company once they grabbed Harkin. His goal was making sure Keane paid for his part in the whole thing, once they eliminated Harkin as a threat. "You have details on the house for the takedown?"

Porter stood and Franks followed suit. "We have it at the office. Call your partner. We'll get all the paperwork in order. Join us there in an hour and we'll lay out the plan. This guy goes down today."

"WHY IS THIS taking so long?" Juliette paced back and forth in Andre's living room. She knew she should sit down and try to make small talk with his brothers, whom Andre had called to stay with her while he went after Harkin. But every time she tried to relax, she got so jittery she had to move.

She remembered this feeling somewhat from her days being married to Dylan, but it had been different. She'd known his job as a cop was dangerous, but he'd always brushed her off when she wanted details. It might have made her worry less, but it left her feeling disconnected, too. Not Andre. When she asked him something, he told her the truth, even if it wasn't what she wanted to hear.

"It's only been fifteen minutes since he left," Marcos said, amusement in his voice. "He probably hasn't even reached the WFO yet."

"Just relax," Cole said, in his ever-calm voice.

"My brother has a ton of training. He's good at what he does. He's going to be fine."

Logically, she knew that. Andre had told her about his training, which was so intense that it was actually a regular part of his job duties. The guy had even trained with most of the military's Special Operations teams. He was more than qualified to take down Harkin.

Emotionally, though, she couldn't stop dwelling on all the little things that could go wrong. In a job as dangerous as his, there were so many variables.

She vaguely heard Marcos ask Cole, "Distraction?"

Cole responded, "Distraction." Then, they were guiding her over to the couch and putting a photo book in her hands.

"What's this?"

"Open it," Marcos said. "I guarantee you it will keep you occupied for a little while."

Curious, she flipped open the cover and then she felt a smile stretch her lips. On the first page were two pictures. She recognized the subjects in the first one immediately: it was a shot of Andre, Cole and Marcos as young boys. They were almost scrawny and wore mud-splattered clothes as if they'd been playing sports right before the shot had been taken. The three stood in a row, their arms looped over one another's shoulders.

"What's this one?" She tapped the other picture on the page.

"That's Andre as a baby," Cole said.

She studied the two people holding him and realized she should have known it instantly. Although the image was yellowed with age and wrinkled, as though it had been carried around in a pocket for years, Andre had his mother's eyes and his father's dimple.

She stared at it for a while, then flipped to the next page, finding more images of him with Cole and Marcos, a little bit older. "You sure Andre won't mind me looking through this?"

Cole gave her a smile she couldn't quite interpret, other than she knew it had something to do with patience. "Of course not."

"You do know my brother is cr—" Marcos cut off midway as Cole elbowed him.

Juliette lifted her gaze from the photo album. "He's what?"

Marcos was obviously trying hard not to roll his eyes at Cole. "Nothing. Hey, Andre said that graphic design wasn't really your first job choice, but you picked it because you were qualified and it wouldn't be a way for your ex to track you."

"Smart," Cole said. "Old habits and unusual activities are one of the ways people who are hiding get tracked down. Well, that and money and hits on your social security number."

"So, what did you do before you moved here?" Marcos asked.

"I was an artist back in Pennsylvania. Oil paintings mostly. I did a bit of everything, but my favorite was portraits," Juliette said, and it felt like a lifetime ago that she'd held a paintbrush in her hands and stood in front of a canvas. She missed the slightly toxic smell of the paints, the calluses on her fingers from holding a brush for so many hours, the pride of finally getting a painting right after working on it for days or weeks.

"You loved it," Marcos said. "I can tell. So, when this is all over, will you go back to painting? We have a lot of good galleries in DC."

Cole tried to elbow him again, but Marcos dodged the hit.

"Uh, I don't know." If things didn't work out between her and Andre, could she bear to stay here? Virginia had never really felt like home, but all of a sudden, she didn't want to leave.

She'd spent most of her time here afraid to do things. Although she'd stopped constantly looking over her shoulder, she hadn't dared to even take a community art class, because she'd been too afraid Dylan would find some way to track her if she did. It might have seemed paranoid, and maybe it was, but he'd found her too many times before when she was sure she'd buried all her tracks.

She'd avoided getting too close to anyone, so they wouldn't probe into her past. She hated lying to people. And without a lot of friends, she hadn't done much socially. So, Virginia had just been the place she lived—and in the back of her mind, she'd always expected it to be one more spot on her list, another place she'd have to leave when Dylan inevitably tracked her down again.

The idea that her need to run might really, truly come to an end felt suddenly overwhelming. No matter what she did, she'd need to start over. It was just a question of how much of a fresh start she wanted.

Would it be enough to simply find a new place to live around here, a new job? Or did she need to go somewhere truly new, a place untainted by Dylan and her own fear?

She thought back to the moment it all started, when she'd been in that club in Pennsylvania, just a year out of school and out celebrating her first painting in a show. Dylan had shown up and asked her out and she'd hesitated, her internal warning system blaring that something wasn't quite right. But she'd shrugged it off and agreed to that first date, and a year later, they were married.

She wondered now if subconsciously she'd

known it was too coincidental that he'd been there that night, right after pulling her over, when she'd never seen him before that day. Maybe some part of her had realized he'd tracked her down, had known she should be wary.

Now, her internal warning system was going again, but with Andre, it was totally different. She'd never felt scared or uncertain about him. She'd only been concerned about herself.

She'd thought that, because of her choice with Dylan before, she couldn't trust her own judgment. But maybe the real problem was that she was afraid of herself: of her own shortcomings, of taking a big chance on another relationship and having it end. Of what that might say about *her*.

The realization didn't make her any less certain about what she was supposed to do when it came to Andre or her future, but it did make her wish she hadn't asked him to wait last night. Because today, he was off on a mission for her, and no matter what his brothers said about his skills, no matter what she'd seen firsthand, it was still dangerous.

What if he didn't make it back today and the last thing she'd told him about their future was that she didn't know how she felt? Because the truth was hitting her hard now. As much as it scared her, she knew exactly how she felt:

somehow, she'd managed to fall in love with him. Now, she just had to figure out what to do about it.

"A NIGHTTIME ENTRY would have been the better option for this," Scott whispered to Andre as the sedan they were riding in pulled onto the long road leading up to the house where Harkin was hiding.

Andre shrugged. He agreed—since Harkin was a murder suspect, and one they knew to be armed, breaching the house silently while they expected him to be asleep would have been the most logical approach. And despite his desire to take Harkin down as swiftly as possible, he'd backed his partner up when Scott had pressed that point back at the WFO office.

But Franks and Porter wanted to go in now. They'd argued that with a failed attempt on Quantico behind him, they couldn't be sure how long Harkin would stay. They worried if he ran, it could lead to an arrest in an area with more civilians present. At least here, they knew he was contained and almost certainly alone, with no risk of anyone getting in the crossfire if Harkin decided to go out shooting.

But every one of them wanted to bring him in alive. They needed Harkin if they wanted answers. And Andre desperately wanted answers, for Juliette.

"It's one guy," Porter snapped, obviously having the hearing of a bat. "You two should be jumping up and down that we invited you along."

"Oh, we are," Scott said, in such an even tone that Andre could tell Porter wasn't sure if he was being mocked or not.

They'd also considered a ruse approach—having an agent knock on the door dressed as a utility worker—but rejected it as too risky with a suspect who'd killed a law enforcement officer. Instead, they were going with a dynamic entry. It was HRT's specialty: speed, surprise and violence of action.

But today, as Franks pulled the sedan to a stop far enough from the house that Harkin wouldn't see them coming, a bad feeling came over Andre. He had no idea why, since he'd done this kind of entry plenty of times, both in practice and for real. He could practically run it blindfolded.

Franks and Porter pulled on the rest of their gear, and Andre stepped out with Scott to do the same. "Be careful," he told them all and although Scott and Franks nodded back at him, Porter rolled his eyes.

"Let's do this," Porter said.

They ran crouched low just behind the tree

line until they were close to the front door. Then they paused only a moment until each man nodded he was ready to go. With a quick hand signal, Andre led them to the front door, racing forward as fast as he could with the battering ram.

With one hard slam, the door split from its hinges and fell into the house. Then, Andre was racing in after it, praying the sudden premonition he'd gotten that something was going to go very wrong wouldn't come true.

Chapter Fifteen

"Move, move, move!" Andre yelled, clearing the doorway fast. It was the most dangerous place in a breach, because until you were through it, you had nowhere to move and you were in a clear line of sight if the suspect expected you.

Then he was moving to the right and Scott cleared behind him, breaking left. A few seconds later, Porter was at his back, Franks lined up behind Scott and the four of them hurried forward. Every second that they didn't contain Harkin was another second for him to grab a weapon and start shooting.

But as soon as he was standing in the massive living room just inside the front door, Andre knew his premonition had been right. The living room was open, with funky modern furniture that left nowhere to hide, and it was clear. But the floor plans for the house they'd pored over before breaching, back at the WFO, were wrong.

The owner must have made massive changes since then, and when they'd spoken to her, she hadn't mentioned it. So, the FBI didn't have the new design.

"New plan," Scott said, eyeing the split-level staircase directly beyond the living room. It had been located at the back of the house in the plans they'd seen.

"You take downstairs," Andre said. "Porter and I will keep moving forward through the first floor. Advise us when you're on your way back up." It was the only way to continue the breach without giving Harkin an opportunity to sneak up on them.

Scott nodded, barely looking fazed as he led Franks slowly down the stairway ahead of them. But he and Scott had thousands of hours of training in this kind of search. A regular special agent would get plenty of training at the Academy, but whether they did any afterward depended on where they ended up. Porter's expression was hard, his hands too tight on the grip of his pistol, as Andre glanced back at him, nodding toward the hallway.

"We move fast," Andre reminded him, taking the lead. He had to trust that Porter was behind him, against the opposite wall of the hallway, and ready for the takedown, however it happened.

It felt like minutes, but Andre knew only seconds passed as they rushed down the hallway, fast enough to keep the element of surprise but slow enough to watch for threats. Beyond the short hallway was a kitchen, and if more changes hadn't been made, then there should be a family room to the right of it.

The turn out of the hallway was another dangerous point, a spot where they had no visual. So Andre pulled out a small mirror and held it just past the edge of the hallway, and his pulse instantly picked up. "Family room, behind a chair. He's armed," Andre whispered, both to Porter coming up beside him and over the mic so Scott and Franks could hear.

"Downstairs is clear," Scott replied. "We're coming back up."

Andre kept the mirror steady, happy Harkin hadn't spotted it. But he'd heard them break down the door, and he was definitely on edge, crouched behind the cover of a big recliner, a gun peeking out, held in shaky hands.

"There's a mudroom behind the family room," Andre said. "Another entrance." He wasn't sure why Harkin hadn't tried to escape that way, but maybe he'd correctly assumed they'd catch up to him before he got far, since his vehicle was parked out front and behind the house was a stretch of open land. It was why they hadn't bothered stationing anyone at the back or blocking the exit before going in.

"Heading toward you now," Scott said.

"Great. I want you to join Porter. I'm going to go around to the mudroom. When I say go, draw his attention. I'll rush him."

"I can go that way," Scott replied.

Although Andre knew it made more sense, he wanted to do this. He needed to be the one to take Harkin down—and to be sure they brought the guy in alive—for Juliette. "I got it."

"Affirmative," Scott replied, and then Andre nodded at him as they traded places. Porter followed him back the way they'd come and around the side of the house.

"I want you out here, guarding the rear exit," Andre told him.

Porter opened his mouth, but then snapped it shut and gave a quick nod.

It was better for one person to make a clandestine entrance than two. Andre slid his pistol into the holster strapped to his thigh and tested the handle on the door to the mudroom. It was locked, so he pulled out his kit and quickly opened it, then slid into the house.

"In five," he whispered to Scott over his mic, then stepped forward, placing his feet slowly so there'd be no unexpected creaks. He slid to the edge of the mudroom and waited, not daring to even peer around the edge.

He knew where Harkin was. It was up to Scott to keep his attention focused the other way.

He counted down the remaining seconds in his head, then the instant he heard a loud *thump* from the front of the house—as though Scott had slammed his fist into the wall—Andre darted around the corner.

A gun went off, close enough to make his ears hurt, and he landed on Harkin, slamming him into the ground and wrapping both of his hands around Harkin's gun hand. The force of the hit briefly knocked the air from his lungs as Harkin bucked wildly, trying to break free.

Andre smashed Harkin's hand down until his grip broke, and the gun slipped away from him. Andre swept his hand out, shoving it farther out of Harkin's reach, then got his feet back underneath him and yanked Harkin's hands behind his back.

Harkin's head snapped back, almost head butting Andre, and made him lose his grip. Faster than he'd expected, Harkin rolled over, then aimed an uppercut at Andre.

Out of his peripheral vision, he saw Scott run into the room and scoop up Harkin's weapon as Andre jumped back, avoiding the hit. Then he rushed back in before Harkin could recover, using the man's own momentum to propel him forward into the wall.

"You're under arrest," Andre barked, snapping handcuffs on him before he could resist again.

"It's over," Franks said, sounding excited. Andre shoved Harkin forward so they could get him in a car and back to the FBI's holding area for questioning.

"Not quite," Scott said.

"We still need to find Keane," Andre added, watching Harkin's expression.

His face spasmed, then he seemed to collect himself as he demanded, "I want my lawyer."

"You're going to need one," Scott said. "Because we're planning to match casings from Quantico to your rifle downstairs."

There was no response, but Andre could see it in the heavy breath Harkin let out. They were going to match.

Scott grabbed a fistful of Harkin's sleeve and passed him over to Franks as Porter finally came in through the mudroom. "Hang on to him." Then, he nodded at Andre. "You need to come downstairs and see something."

Andre gave one backward glance at Harkin, who looked as though he'd swallowed something foul, and then followed Scott down to the lower level.

They passed a large, open area set up with a

bar and seating that would have been quick for Scott and Franks to clear, then went into a small office tucked away in the back. Scott gestured at the wall above the desk.

Pinned to the wall were pictures, dozens of them. All of Juliette.

"WHY DID YOU have pictures of Mya Moreau?" Porter demanded, slamming his hands on the table in the interview room where Harkin was sitting, his lawyer beside him.

It took a minute for Andre to remember they were talking about Juliette. It was strange to hear anyone use her given name, instead of the name she'd given herself. He leaned forward, practically pressing his nose against the one-way glass, watching for Harkin's reaction.

They'd been back at the Washington Field Office for two hours, and although Harkin wasn't being very cooperative, they expected that to change very soon. The rifle they'd found upstairs at the house where Harkin had been hiding was expected to be a match to the casings they'd found at the scene.

They had a firearms examiner testing it now: every casing spent from a rifle left unique markings from the barrel, and they'd soon know if this rifle was a match to the casings found outside of Quantico. When that came back positive, which Andre knew it would, Harkin would be itching to make a deal.

And Andre wanted a reason for officers in Leming, Pennsylvania, to knock on the door of the cabin where Keane was holed up and arrest him. He wished he could be there to do it himself, but it would have to be satisfaction enough to have the man behind bars.

"They're not my pictures," Harkin said stubbornly, shaking his head as his lawyer whispered something in his ear.

"So it's just coincidental that she was at Quantico when you tried to shoot the place up? And that she was the intended target of a hit you ordered on a marketing company?" Franks asked.

"And it's coincidental she witnessed you making a payoff to a police officer in return for not bringing you in on a murder charge?" Porter added.

Harkin scowled, but beneath the anger Andre saw the hint of fear in his eyes. He hadn't realized how much the FBI knew.

"This could be a while," Scott said from where he was stretched out on a chair across the room, snacking on a handful of chocolate candy.

"Yeah, I know. You don't have to wait around," Andre said.

"It's okay. Chelsie's out with my sister tonight anyway."

Andre glanced back at his partner, who'd changed in the time since he'd met his fiancée, Chelsie. There was a new sense of calm happiness about him that Andre envied—and he knew that same kind of peace was within his reach. He just needed to see this case wrapped up and then find a way to convince Juliette that they were better off together than apart.

In the adjoining room, Porter's voice carried loudly as he added, almost conversationally, "You know, when we're finished examining the rifle, we're going to check out that pistol you fired today at FBI agents. I'm betting that comes back as matching the bullet that killed a police officer in Pennsylvania."

Harkin's lawyer leaned forward once more, whispering in his ear, and Harkin jerked away, then stared down at the table for a long moment. Finally, he gave his lawyer a defeated nod.

The lawyer leaned forward. "We want to make a deal."

THE INSTANT THE door opened and Andre stepped inside, Juliette could tell something was wrong.

She jumped up from the couch, setting aside his photo book, and ran over to him, inspecting him from head to toe until she could be certain he wasn't injured. Once she confirmed he seemed fine physically, some of the worry eased. "What happened?"

"We got him. Harkin confessed in exchange for a deal. Assuming his story checks out and his testimony helps, he'll get some concessions on his sentence—where he serves it and for how long, maybe more."

"That's good news, right?" Marcos asked as he and Cole joined them in the entryway.

Andre took her hand, holding on to it like she was going to need support. "Let's sit down."

Uneasy, Juliette let him lead her back to the couch. She watched him take in the discarded photo album without comment. Once they were all seated again, everyone watched Andre expectantly.

"The takedown went okay?" Cole asked, wearing an expression Juliette could only describe as big brotherly.

She had a sudden wish for family in her life who would stand by her the way Andre's brothers stood by him. Her gaze swiveled from Cole to Marcos and then back to Andre. They'd been there for her, just because Andre had asked. If she and Andre worked out, she'd be gaining a real family. If they didn't, she'd be losing more than just a relationship—and hurting more than one person.

Pushing that worry aside for later, she added, "No one was injured, right?"

"Nah, everyone is fine," Andre replied.

Her heart rate should have gone back to normal, but she could tell bad news was still coming.

"The takedown went mostly as planned. A few snafus but nothing huge. We got Harkin back to the field office and matched the casings from the rifle used at Quantico to the one found in the house."

"So, it *was* him at Quantico." It had seemed to be the only option, with Dylan in Pennsylvania and Jim dead before the incident happened, but it was good to have it confirmed. And if he'd admitted to firing at federal agents—whether or not they had been his actual target—Juliette knew jail time was in his future.

"Yeah. And he fired when we were inside the house." Juliette must have looked a little panicked, because Andre added quickly, "A rogue shot. Didn't hit anyone. Anyway, that pistol is being checked now. We were pretty confident we were going to match it to the bullet used to kill Valance, so the agents brought it up and Harkin's only option was to get ahead of what he could."

"Okay," Juliette said, trying not to fidget as Andre shifted to face her, gripping her hand just a little tighter.

"He admitted to killing Jim Valance and to the shooting at Quantico."

In the chairs across from them, Andre's brothers were silent and Juliette said what they had to all be thinking. "But not to hiring the convicts to kill me? He's saying that was Dylan, isn't he?" That had to be why Andre looked so worried about her.

The idea hurt, especially after starting to have doubts over the past few days that Dylan had ever really tried to kill her, but the truth was that she'd spent three years thinking it, so it wasn't exactly a new concept. Besides, whether or not he'd tried to have her killed, there was no doubt that he'd terrorized her over the years. And if she really wanted to put her past behind her, she needed to find a way to accept that Dylan's mistakes were his own. Even if a tiny piece of her still felt responsible for marrying him in the first place.

"That's not all," Andre said. "What he's claiming is that his murder of Jim Valance was self-defense, and that the shooting in Quantico was during a time when he was temporarily insane."

Cole snorted. "That's pretty convenient. He's not even going to wait until trial to bring up temporary insanity, huh? Just get it on the table now."

"Why would anyone believe that?" Juliette

asked, her nervousness increasing with every minute. She wasn't sure where this was going, but she knew it wasn't good. Not for Dylan and probably not for her, either.

"Harkin's story is that during the investigation into Manning's murder, Valance and Keane questioned him repeatedly, getting more aggressive each time. He says that eventually, they coerced him into a payoff, saying otherwise they'd plant evidence for a murder he didn't commit."

"No way!" Juliette interrupted. "I heard him at my house. He didn't sound coerced at all. And Jim wasn't even there."

"Well, according to him, that payoff came *after* they'd made the demand and he'd agreed. He said they were just reiterating what had already been agreed. He says he has no idea if Loews is actually guilty, and he doesn't know why Keane told him there was nothing he could do for Loews."

"That makes no sense," Juliette argued, but as she looked from Andre to his brothers and back, she could tell Harkin's story had planted doubt about the way they'd assumed everything had gone down.

Andre's fingers stroked her palm. "We're still trying to verify all of this, but Harkin's claim does have some internal logic. I think he's lying about some of it, but honestly, the most believable lies tend to be mixed with the truth, and I think at least some of what he's saying is true."

She started to argue, but he continued, "Harkin says that Keane and Valance continued to harass him after Loews went to jail, demanding more money every few months or they'd 'find' new evidence and try to reopen the case, then name him as a coconspirator. Harkin claims that recently Valance demanded a meeting in a deserted warehouse. Harkin was afraid Valance was going to kill him because he'd been asking for more money and Harkin had refused to make the most recent payoff. He says they argued and that he'd only brought the gun for self-protection, but Valance tried to take it, and it went off by accident."

"Wasn't he shot in the head?" Cole interjected.

"Yeah, so that story is probably twisted to his benefit," Andre said, then turned to Juliette again. "He also says Keane told him you'd overheard him making a payoff and that you needed to disappear for good."

Juliette felt herself jerk at the news, a whole new level of betrayal rushing through her, which was ridiculous. If Dylan had tried to kill her, if he'd sent *hit men* to try to kill her, what did it matter if he'd also sent a murderer like Harkin after her? But somehow, she felt blindsided.

"He had pictures of you at the house he was staying in here. A lot of them."

Juliette felt her hand tighten around Andre's until she knew she was gripping way too hard, but he didn't seem bothered. "What kind of pictures?"

"Shots from a lot of different states over the years. The writing on the back labeling the places doesn't match Harkin's. We suspect it's Keane's, since you already confirmed you'd seen him following you."

She nodded, feeling as though she was in a daze. "Dylan gave them to Harkin to help him find me?"

"We're not sure. That's what Harkin is saying, but it's also possible he stole them. He says he didn't know where you were until he saw news of the hostage situation online and recognized your picture. Then, he claims he panicked, sure that since Keane's hit men had failed, Keane would take it out on him. He says that drove him temporarily crazy, and he came here. He saw that agents from Quantico had been at the scene, so he waited at Quantico, hoping to see you. That's when he took the shots."

"And you're buying all of this?" Juliette asked, not sure what to think of Harkin's story.

"Some of it," Andre replied.

"From what Andre said, the things Harkin

admitted to are basically what he knew the FBI could connect him to forensically," Marcos said.

"Exactly," Andre agreed. "He's trying to put the best spin he can on what he knows we're going to be able to prove, and put the rest on Keane. But that doesn't necessarily mean he's lying. There's consistency to the story, and it didn't sound rehearsed."

"So, what's next? How do we figure out if his story is true?" Juliette asked.

"Officers in Leming are bringing Keane in as we speak," Andre said. "We should have his side of the story anytime now."

As if on cue, Andre's phone rang and his eyebrows lifted. "It's the case agents. I'm hoping they're going to bring Keane here for questioning, but if not, I requested to fly down with them to Pennsylvania to be involved in it." He picked up the phone. "Diaz."

Juliette loosened her hold on his hand just a little as he spoke. The pieces of Harkin's story swirled in her mind, and even though she knew some of it had to be simply about saving himself, parts of it *did* sound like the truth. After all the years of being sure Dylan was out to get her, and then the few days of uncertain hope that maybe her instincts about her ex-husband hadn't been entirely disastrous, disappointment crashed in on her.

Then Andre hung up the phone, his grim expression filling her with dread. "Keane is gone."

Chapter Sixteen

It had been twenty-four hours and there was still no sign of Keane.

"How did this happen?" Andre tried to keep the frustration out of his voice, but it rang through clearly.

Marcos shook his head, angrier than Andre had seen him in a long time. "I don't know. Kendry was watching him. Keane must have known it. Honestly, he was probably counting on it, so everyone was distracted, thinking they knew where he was. It gave him a head start." His gaze jumped to Juliette. "I'm sorry. I honestly thought we had him pretty contained."

"So did his department," Andre said, not wanting Marcos to feel responsible. "Everyone was confident about that."

"It's not your fault," Juliette said. "But how did he get out? Do they know how long he's been gone? They were checking often, right? So they must have a window when his car disappeared."

"Well, that's just it. He fooled them all. He set automatic timers in the house so the lights went on and off at expected times. And his car is still there, right out in front of the cabin. They don't know how he slipped past them, but the cabin is in the woods, so he could have gone on foot. We have no idea how long he's been gone. The last time Kendry saw him personally was when he checked in at the station a few days ago. The cop who checked on him after the Quantico shooting just checked the outside, didn't actually speak to Keane."

"He couldn't have gone far on foot. If he stole a vehicle, that should have popped up by now," Cole said, his shoulders slumped as he downed his third coffee in as many hours.

Since Andre had made the coffee, he knew Cole had to be wiped out to be drinking so much without a word of complaint. All of them were exhausted. His brothers had been at his house practically nonstop between working, and the strain was starting to show. But he knew they wouldn't have it any other way: the three of them always stuck together.

"Yeah," Andre agreed, downing the rest of his own coffee even though it had long ago gone cold. "I bet he had a vehicle waiting nearby. He had this well planned."

"But what's his next goal?" Marcos asked, and everyone turned to Juliette.

She shook her head, obviously bewildered. "It makes the most sense that he's going to just try to disappear, right? Try to outrun the investigation?"

Her voice held a mix of hope and doubt, and Andre knew why. Keane had spent so many years tracking her; would he give up now?

"The most logical answer is that he's had this planned for years," Cole said. "He set up a failsafe, a way out if the situation with Harkin ever became public. Obviously he knew it was possible, between Valance demanding more money from Harkin and you out there somewhere, knowing the truth. As a cop, you get caught doing *half* the things we suspect Keane of, and you're in serious trouble. No cop wants to end up behind bars, with the people they put away."

Juliette looked a little nauseous and Andre wasn't sure if it was the idea of some criminal coming after her ex-husband in jail or simply the idea that Keane was still out there somewhere, unaccounted for.

The way he always did when she seemed worried, he slid his hand across the small space separating them on the couch and wove his fingers through hers. He wasn't sure when the action had become so natural, almost instinctual, but it must have been for her, too, because her hand curled into his before she glanced at their connected hands. She smiled up at him, seeming almost surprised.

"Shaye never found the trail of money to pay those cons," Marcos interjected. "Wherever that money came from could be his backup funds if he had to run."

"The FBI didn't find it either," Cole said, "but Shaye's still searching."

"Isn't that going to be a dead end?" Juliette asked. "I'm sure he was smart enough to use cash."

"Sure," Cole agreed, "but that much cash? Even if he didn't take it all out at once, we should see something that lines up. Anyway, Shaye's stopped hunting it from Keane's end and now she's trying to go from the criminals, tracking their payment backward. That might work better if Keane used a fake name to set up the account, which he probably did."

"The case agents are still hunting for that trail, too," Andre said. "They're also arranging interviews with just about everyone in Keane's life, from his family to his coworkers, trying to find places he could consider safe or contacts who might help him." He'd gotten off the phone with them a few minutes ago, and they'd both sounded discouraged, their resources spread too thin.

A police detective who'd spent a decade on the force would know all the tricks. He'd know how to avoid detection. And it sounded as though he already had a fake identity set up, that he'd been planning this all along.

"Chances are, his goal is to get out of the country," Cole said. "His best bet is to go somewhere without extradition."

"If he makes it, we might never know," Juliette said. Andre could tell what she was thinking: her days of hiding might never end.

"He's not going to make it," Andre vowed.

Keane had managed to stay one step ahead of them so far, but now the FBI's attention wasn't split among Valance and Harkin and Keane. Now, the focus was solely on Keane. And Andre wasn't giving up until he was behind bars and Juliette was free from this nightmare.

"WELL, I'VE GOT good news and bad news," Cole announced. He emerged from Andre's kitchen after taking a call from Shaye.

Juliette felt like she'd been on a roller coaster the past few days. Everything seemed to be two steps forward and one step back, except when it came to Dylan. Then, it was the opposite.

Cole and Marcos had slept on Andre's pullout couch last night, sticking close in case something broke and they were needed. Ever since they'd learned Dylan had gone missing yesterday, everyone seemed to be on high alert.

Juliette had no idea if Andre's brothers were off work anyway or if they'd taken days off for this. She hardly knew what day it was anymore. Everything had become a blur of investigations, and her past and her future tangled together as though they were never going to break apart.

"What is it?" Andre asked. In the past day, his constantly optimistic attitude had started to slip a little, and even he was starting to show the strain of trying to battle her demons for her.

He hadn't asked for this. She'd waited for him at Quantico that day because he'd been nice to her. Not even so much because he'd been the one to save her life when the gunman had led her out of her office, but because she'd instinctively known he wouldn't hurt her. Even if she held a gun on him and demanded he help her escape.

She wanted to put this behind her, and not just so she could move on with her life, although that was a big part of it. But she wanted the dynamic of their relationship to change, too. She wanted to be here with Andre because they both wanted it, and not because he was still trying to protect her. It was time for her to be his equal, and not a pawn in her ex-husband's schemes.

"Are you okay?" Andre asked, and she realized they'd all been staring at her.

She blinked, trying to clear whatever expression had been on her face, and nodded as she waited to hear what her ex had done now.

"Shaye tracked the money."

"That's great news," Juliette said, surprised. "That means, what? She figured out what name he used? Can't we try to track him with that?" She glanced from Andre to Marcos, thinking it was a good lead and wondering what she was missing. But they were just staring expectantly at Cole and she remembered she hadn't heard the bad news yet.

"Looks like Keane didn't use cash. He sent wire transfers and Shaye tracked it back from the criminals' accounts. Keane set up an account with a fake name and paid the cons out of it for the hit."

"Is she sure it was Dylan?" Juliette asked softly.

"Yeah," Cole said. "I'm sorry. Shaye hacked the bank's security. We've got a picture of him that lines up exactly with when the wire transfer was sent. She confirmed it all. We can't use it in court, but it's him."

So there was no question. Juliette expected to

feel surprise, or even sadness, at the final confirmation that her husband had been the one to put out the hit on her, but somehow, all she felt was numb. The weight on the couch shifted as Andre scooted closer and slid his arm around her shoulders and she leaned into him, waiting for the rest of it.

"Apparently, this account was only set up a few months ago. The money that went into it was probably the payoffs from Harkin. Shaye's guess is that he kept it as cash until recently. Not smart to hoard that much cash, but—"

"He had a good hiding spot," Juliette said. "He always said he trusted a hidey hole more than a bank."

"With someone like Shaye on your trail, that's probably a good instinct," Cole said.

"That woman is a genius if she's on your side and a serious threat if she's not," Marcos said. "Especially if she's working outside the law."

"Yeah," Cole agreed, but he seemed guilt-stricken about asking her to go outside the law. "Anyway, that would line up with what Harkin was saying about Valance demanding more money lately. We've confirmed that Valance was having money troubles because of a gambling problem. So, Keane might have realized the whole thing was going to go south on him and it was time to take action."

"So, we still don't know if he was chasing after me for three years to kill me or drag me back," Juliette said, although she wondered if it really mattered now.

"No. What we do know is that Keane paid the three cons out of this account and he had plenty left to start over. Before Shaye could tag the account, he transferred the rest of the money. She knows it went overseas, but she can't find it."

"It sure sounds as though he's trying to run," Marcos said.

"No." Cole's expression was troubled as he looked at Juliette. "Right before he transferred the rest of the money, Keane withdrew a bunch of cash. He did it in Maryland, just outside Washington, DC, earlier today."

Andre's hold on her tightened.

"He's in Maryland?" she repeated.

"He was three hours ago," Cole replied.

"He's close," Marcos said unnecessarily.

"Yeah, but why is it taking him so long?" Andre wondered. "He slipped away from Leming more than twenty-four hours ago. He could have been staking out her apartment by now."

"He's coming in slowly, maybe going through DC instead of passing it by because it's an unexpected route," Cole said. He nodded as if that's the way he'd do it if he were on the run. "He's being careful."

"Then, he's not leaving the country," Andre said. "At least not without making a stop first. Because we're on pretty high alert for him in Virginia and DC. He has to know that he'd be better off making a run for it by heading the other way."

"He's got everything ready to run, but he's going to come here and eliminate me first." Juliette said the words everyone else was dancing around.

"He'll be caught before he makes it anywhere near you," Cole said. "Every officer and agent within a hundred miles is watching for him. It's harder than you think to slip through that kind of net."

"He got this close," Juliette said. "You said he's right outside of DC already." Really, what Cole had said was that Dylan had been outside of DC three hours ago. For all they knew, he was here now, waiting for her to go home.

"Even if he could get close," Marcos contributed, "he's not going to be able to track you to Andre's house. And just in case, by some crazy fluke he manages to get Andre's name, we can move you somewhere with no connection to my brother. We'll stay away from FBI resources totally and use a DEA safe house. We can move you within the hour."

"Even if he found us," Andre said, gripping

each of her arms and staring intently at her, projecting total confidence, "he'd never get past me."

A smile trembled on her lips, but she couldn't hold it. "I've put you in danger long enough."

"*You* haven't put me in danger at all," Andre said, so quickly she knew he actually believed it.

"I don't want you to have to stand in front of me. Any of you." She'd come to know all of them pretty well over the past few days. Any one of them would put his life on the line for her, and if any of them were hurt protecting her, it would be far worse than Dylan catching up to her, whatever his intentions.

"It won't come to that," Andre said, but something in his voice told her he almost wanted to face Dylan one on one.

"I'll take the FBI up on the safe house they offered me. I want to be far away from you if he does manage to evade everyone."

Andre pulled her close, hugging her against him so tightly it was almost hard to breathe. "That'll never work. I'll just volunteer to be on your protection detail."

"I just think it's safer for everyone—"

"It's not going to happen," Andre cut her off.

"Okay," Juliette said as a whole new plan flashed through her mind, a plan she knew would end this, one way or another. And it was long past time to take her life back. "Then I know a way we can draw Dylan out and finish this."

She leaned back, pulling out of Andre's embrace so he could see her eyes, see that she wasn't going to back down about this. "We use me as bait."

Chapter Seventeen

"That is never going to happen." Andre put his hands on his hips, using the glare he usually saved for uncooperative suspects.

It should have made Juliette back down, but instead her lips trembled as if he'd said something funny.

"I'm not kidding," he snapped, keeping his voice near a whisper even though he knew it made him seem less intimidating. His brothers were sleeping in the next room, and he didn't want to wake them.

Ever since Juliette had announced her dangerous plan earlier that evening, she'd been stuck on it, ticking off all the reasons it was their best chance for bringing Keane down and sounding way too logical. He, on the other hand, had come off as too emotionally invested. But bless his brothers, they'd taken his side.

Still, Juliette hadn't given up, and after his

brothers had finally announced they needed to call it a night, she'd dragged him into the guest room to keep pushing her case.

"Everyone is out there searching for him. You flaunting yourself as bait isn't going to change the end result. We'll catch him, and we'll do it without putting you in unnecessary danger."

"Andre," Juliette said softly, still so calm it was starting to piss him off. "What happens if he gets here and he can't find me? What happens if he gives up and he uses whatever fake name he's cooked up and goes overseas, somewhere you can't bring him back? I want this to be over. I want him to pay for the things he's done."

"So do I," Andre said. "But not if it means exposing you to danger."

"I'll be fine," she insisted. "I'm not planning to run screaming down the streets until he finds me alone. We'll set it up so the FBI is watching me. He comes close, and you guys arrest him and bring him in."

"If it's too easy, he'll suspect a setup and disappear," Andre said, trying to sound reasonable. The truth was, if he spotted a setup, he'd probably still come. If Keane was willing to risk all the heat in Virginia to get back at his ex-wife, he'd willingly walk into a setup, too, as long as he thought he could outwit them. And with someone confident enough to think he'd get away with all the things he'd done already, Andre had no doubt Keane believed he could.

The problem was, even if they had all the advantages, there was one scenario that no law enforcement agent wanted to face, because it was a no-win. It didn't matter how much protection they put around Juliette if Keane was willing to trade his own life to take her out. And if things seemed dire enough, he might hit that point. Andre wasn't willing to take the risk.

"You know that if we give him a chance to grab me, he'll try," Juliette said and she didn't look scared about what that meant.

"What if we set you up as bait and he just shoots you?" Andre asked harshly. "At this point, he may not care if you see him first. He sent hit men in to take you out, remember?"

She blinked, and he saw a hint of fear behind the determination. "It's a chance I'm willing to take."

"Well, I'm not."

"Andre." She pulled his hand off his hip and held it with both of hers, sparks of determination in her hazel eyes. "This is my life. I need to be able to live it again, without this shadow hanging over everything I ever do. If it means I have to put myself in danger, I'm okay with that. I need to be free of this, and I need to help bring him down."

Andre tried to interrupt, but she kept going. "After everything he did, to so many people, I need to finally take a stand. I can't keep hiding and hope someone else takes care of this problem for me. Can't you understand that?"

Fear clenched his chest, because he *could* understand it. The fact was, it was exactly what he'd be doing if he were in her position.

"I don't like it," he muttered and cursed himself silently, because it sounded as if he was giving in.

"I know," she said, stepping closer and keeping hold of his hand. "But I trust you to keep me safe. I'm ready to be free from this fear." She gazed up at him, only inches away now. "So that we can move forward."

He didn't know if it was a promise for what the future held for the two of them or not. Instead of asking, he tugged her closer still, pulling her flush against him. He didn't give her a chance to explain, just slipped his arms around her and lowered his mouth to hers.

She rose up on her tiptoes, looping her arms around his neck. She kissed him back, picking up the pace instantly.

He slowed them down, keeping his arms tight around her when she would have pulled his shirt off, pressing his lips along the column of her throat until she whimpered. He stayed there for a long time, until she was squirming in his arms, before he finally brought his lips back to hers.

Her hands slid up underneath his T-shirt. Her nails dug into his back as he stroked her tongue with his, trying to tell her without words what she meant to him. He forced himself to keep the pace slow, but she moved as though she was trying to get even closer to him. His hands seemed to act without permission, sliding down over the curve of her butt.

She arched up even higher on her tiptoes, her whole body rubbing against him, until she had to know exactly what she was doing to him. "Andre," she breathed into his mouth.

It was easy to scoot his hands down farther, and he gripped her thighs and lifted her so she could loop her legs around his waist. Then he turned and walked the short distance to the bed, his mind and body battling.

He'd promised her that he'd wait until she had closure on her past before they moved forward. And he knew exactly what she was doing right now, from the frantic, almost desperate taste of her kisses. She was trying to create a memory, in case they didn't have a future. In case her plan failed and her ex-husband killed her.

Determination made him hold her tighter. No matter what it took, he was going to keep her safe. And he was going to prove to her that he deserved her.

He lowered her slowly onto the bed, easing himself on top of her and trapping her wrists up over her head. He slipped free of her too-tantalizing mouth and settled his tongue on her earlobe, trying to gain control as she arched beneath him.

She twisted her head, capturing his mouth again and biting on his bottom lip, making it throb. His eyes closed as she pulled her hands free, yanking his shirt up as high as she could. She dropped her hands back down and slid them under the waistband of his pants.

He rolled over, taking her with him, and laughed at her when she tried unsuccessfully to tug her arms free from underneath him.

"Hey!"

"Let's slow down," he panted. "We have plenty of time."

"Well, I was hoping for a couple of times before your brothers woke up," she said, her cheeks going pink and weakening his resolve.

He groaned and closed his eyes, then opened them again before she could distract him with her mouth. "I meant, we have our whole future ahead of us."

She jerked back slightly, but with her hands underneath him, she couldn't go far.

"I know you said you wanted to wait until this was behind you, and you don't have to make me any promises right now. But I'm going to make you one: when this is over and you're safe—because you will be safe—I'm still going to be here. I know the people in your life have let you down, and I understand why you're nervous and even why you might not want to jump into a relationship, but I'm willing to wait. I want to be with you, so I'll do whatever you need so we can really give this a shot."

It was more than he'd intended to say. She was staring at him, her mouth moving as if she was about to respond, but she didn't know how.

So, he beat her to it, rolling to his side so she could slip her hands free, then tucking her in close to him. "You don't need to say anything. I just wanted you to know."

He reached over and flipped off the light on the side table, then wrapped his arm back around her. "Tomorrow, if the FBI doesn't have Keane in custody, we'll figure out a plan. Tonight, I just want to lie close to you."

"ARE YOU SURE you want to do this?" Agent Franks asked her.

It was midday and they'd put this off long enough already, hoping someone would catch Dylan before he slipped out of the country.

Andre's jaw was tight, his mouth in a hard line. Juliette knew he wanted her to call it off and either trust the FBI to catch Dylan or accept it if he managed to get away from them again.

But she also knew that if the roles were reversed and this were him, he'd be doing exactly the same thing. "I'm sure."

If it was possible, the dark expression on Andre's face got even more stern, but she also saw pride in his eyes.

There had been a possible sighting of Dylan earlier today, along a back road coming into the county where she lived, and she'd had a brief burst of hope that he'd be caught and she would get a reprieve. But he'd managed to lose the officer tracking him before backup could arrive.

They couldn't find him. But they knew he was close. It was time to do this. Time to end Dylan's hold on her for good, one way or another.

She gazed at Andre, remembering the feel of his arms around her as she'd drifted in and out of sleep last night. When she'd shared a bed with Dylan, she'd always slept on her own side. But with Andre, it felt right to spend the entire night snuggled up against his warmth and his strength. As if she belonged there.

Whatever doubts she'd been having fled. If she couldn't face her past and forge her own future, then she didn't deserve a man like Andre.

She let her gaze sweep the conference room. The case agents, Franks and Porter, were there. They'd been brought in by Andre, since this was their investigation. Andre's brothers were in the room, too, and Juliette knew some kind of special deal had been made to allow their involvement since neither was FBI and neither had jurisdiction. She'd heard the words "task force" and "paperwork" and a lot of grumbling from Porter, but Andre had insisted. Andre's partner, Scott, was supposed to be here, too, but he'd been called in for HRT at the last minute when one of the other team's snipers had fallen ill.

"Let's go over this one more time," Porter said now, bringing her attention back to him.

He'd settled himself at the front of the room, and although technically he was in charge, Andre had devised most of the plan for today. It gave her confidence that Dylan would bite.

The idea of facing her ex again made fear slide through her, but she tried to force it down and focus. This was it. Today was the last day she'd ever run from Dylan.

"We've evacuated your apartment building and replaced a few of the tenants with agents so it doesn't appear too empty," Porter said. "The news report about spotting Keane driving into Maryland and asking citizens to be on the lookout for him is going to air in half an hour. We're hoping that will give him confidence we're going in the wrong direction, get his guard down a little. Then we'll send you home. We're going to have a marked police car out front, because we don't want him thinking it's too easy."

"Meanwhile," Franks took over, "Agent Porter and I will be in the apartments on either side of you. Officer Walker—" he gestured to Cole "—and Agent Costa—" he looked at Marcos "—will be hiding in the apartment with you."

"And I'll be across the street, on the rifle," Andre finished.

She knew he wanted to be in the room with her, and she'd seen the struggle in his eyes as he'd laid out the plan, putting himself farthest away. But she also knew his skills as a sniper. If Dylan got too close and they had to take him out instead of making an arrest, Andre wouldn't miss.

Besides, she knew there was no one he trusted more to watch over her than Cole and Marcos. The three of them had conferred in the living room this morning while she'd been getting dressed and snippets of their conversation had drifted back to her. She'd heard Cole and Marcos assuring Andre she was going to be just fine and she didn't think she'd ever heard Andre sound so nervous as when he'd told them, "Don't let anything happen to her. If you have even a second's doubt it's going to go bad, just be sure you stay out of my line of fire and I'll take him down."

The idea of the man she might want to spend the rest of her life with shooting the man she'd once pledged that same thing to made bile rise up in her throat. She prayed it wouldn't come to that, but she knew Andre would never shoot unless it was a last resort, maybe especially because it was her ex-husband. He'd never want to hurt her.

The thought bounced around in her head and she locked gazes with him, giving him a shaky smile. She knew it was true. No matter what their future held, it was going to be totally different from her life with Dylan. Her ex had always thought of his own needs first and hers had been a distant second. But with Andre, even in the short time she'd known him, she came first.

She wished she'd spoken out loud the words that had been rattling in her brain as she kissed him last night. *I love you.* She stared at him, wishing he could read her mind, wishing she'd told him. Just in case.

Don't think that way, she scolded herself. But as Porter gave the go-ahead and they left the office for the cars that would take them to her apartment, dread settled in her chest and refused to budge.

Dylan had been so determined to kill her that

he'd chased her for three long years. He'd hired hit men to take her out. Even with law enforcement all over the country searching for him and a certain life sentence waiting for him, he was coming after her again. With someone that single-minded, would they be able to stop him?

Andre pressed a kiss to her lips in front of everyone and then she climbed into the car with Agent Porter. He'd be posing as a neighbor dropping her off. Juliette closed her eyes and said a quick prayer. They were about to find out.

Chapter Eighteen

It had only been an hour since Juliette had been back in her apartment, but she'd been antsy since the second she'd walked through the door. Cole and Marcos had arrived ahead of her and were out of sight, in the other room. She was supposed to move around as if she was returning home after a while away, and she wasn't to talk to them just in case Dylan managed to get eyes on her.

Chances were extremely slim that Dylan could see her, because Andre had made agents sweep any building with a view to her apartment. It was probably overkill, but he'd remembered her talking about Dylan being skilled with a rifle and insisted. The building across the street was already empty—they'd confirmed it earlier, but now it was closed off with only Andre inside.

She resisted the urge to peer out her living room window and across the street to the brand-new apartment complex being built. Even knowing where Andre was, she'd never spot him. And that was the point.

Before they'd returned to her apartment, Andre had made her practice what to do if Dylan managed to get inside with a weapon. It was Juliette's job to move him in front of the window and stay out of the line of fire without being obvious. She'd practiced over and over at Andre's house until it felt almost natural.

But Andre had insisted it was a last resort, that it wasn't going to come to that. Chances were almost zero that Dylan would make it past the agents watching throughout the apartment building and get up to her place on the third floor. And if he did, he'd still have to contend with Marcos and Cole, both of whom had arrived looking ready for battle.

She longed to have her phone ring, to have agents tell her it was over, that they'd caught him. With every minute that went by without word, she got more nervous that Dylan would see through their plan and just run. Because if they didn't catch him today, she'd always wonder when he might reappear. How could she pursue a future with Andre if one day Dylan might show up again and take out his wrath on both of them? On their kids?

She froze, the thought taking her by surprise. But for the first time in a long time, she was anticipating a future, and she could actually envision kids with Andre. A little girl with her eyes and Andre's dimple. A little boy with her smile and Andre's cute little nose. Happiness mingled with panic. It was all too much, too fast, as though after putting her life on hold for so long, she was suddenly heading into warp speed.

She settled stiffly on the couch in her living room, trying to act normal. But she couldn't help glancing around the room. It had only been a few days since she'd left this place, thinking she'd return at the end of the day, but it felt like much, much longer.

The room was a boring beige color, from the walls to the carpeting to the counters in the attached kitchen. Her furniture was functional, and there was just one painting hanging on her wall. It was a bright, cheery watercolor she'd picked up at a fair this summer, her first foray back into normalcy. She'd felt so daring when she'd hung it, as though she was making a statement: *this time, maybe I won't have to run.*

Back in Pennsylvania, her walls had been overrun with paintings. When she'd married Dylan and moved into his house, he'd thought it was too much, so she'd only hung half of what she'd owned. But she missed the splashes of color, the quirky oil paintings, some of which were her own.

She clenched her fists. Dylan had taken that from her: not just her ability to feel safe, but her ability to feel like *her*. Even though she was terrified to confront him again, she desperately wanted him to walk through that door, wanted the chance to tell him that he'd underestimated her.

But where was he? She looked at her watch, wondering if they'd given him enough time. Had he seen the news reports? They'd been broadcasted widely. Maybe he'd seen through the trap.

Her gaze drifted from the window, with the shades pulled wide, to the door, locked and bolted just in case. What were they going to do if he didn't show up today? How long would they keep this ruse up, waiting for him?

She didn't know why, but she'd imagined it all happening fast. She'd been so sure that as soon as she returned to her apartment, he'd be there, furious and anxious to eliminate her for good. But she should have known better. Dylan may have been dangerous and too caught up in his own vendettas to take his best course of action and run, but he was still a cop. An ex-cop now, she amended. And he was still smart.

He might want her dead badly enough to return here, but he'd still conduct surveillance on the apartment building first, make a plan for the best way to get to her.

Would he spot the agents? When she'd walked through the building, she'd seen someone doing laundry downstairs and another supposedly getting mail and both appeared to be regular tenants. But she knew the truth. Would he realize it? Did he have some kind of law enforcement radar, since he'd lived that life for so long?

She wondered for the first time what had turned him. She'd initially thought that Harkin had bribed him, maybe even threatened her, and that had been the start of it. But what if Harkin had been telling the truth? What if Dylan had set it up from the beginning?

If he'd taken money before that day, she'd never seen it. Never suspected anything. They hadn't been hard up for money, but they hadn't been flush with it either. If he'd been hiding it away all along, what had he planned to do with it?

It didn't matter now, she told herself, peering through the doorway into her equally bland bedroom, where Marcos and Cole were waiting out of sight. What was she going to do if he didn't show at all? Would she go through her normal routine, go to sleep and get up and…what? She hadn't returned to work after the shooting at her office and she doubted they'd want her back.

Once this was over, she would really be starting fresh. Again. It felt scary, the way it had every time Dylan had caught up to her in yet another town and she'd had to run again. But this time, it felt exciting, too. She'd never had anything to anticipate before, and now there was a lot.

She would go back to painting. She'd been socking away her savings, so she might even wait before going back to work, see if she was still good enough to sell her art. She'd go out with Andre on real dates. She couldn't help the goofy smile she felt on her face as she remembered his words about kissing her goodnight on her porch. She was going to have to find a new place, one with a porch.

But before any of that could happen, she needed Dylan to show. She leaped to her feet, anxious again. Where was he?

JULIETTE LOOKED JUMPY.

Andre studied her through the scope on his rifle, watching as she hopped off the couch in her living room, then paced and sat back down. She'd been that way for the past twenty minutes, as if she was desperately trying to stay still but couldn't take it.

He was feeling antsy himself.

Everything about this setup was right. The layers of protection around Juliette were solid but invisible. He shifted his rifle from left to right, watching the exterior of the building before moving back up to the apartment again.

By all appearances, the apartment building had a normal level of activity, and they'd gotten lucky with the agents Franks and Porter had recruited, because none of them *looked* like agents. The cops in a marked car out front, taking turns reading a paper and watching the front entrance, finished the ruse. It should have led Keane around the back, into Andre's line of sight, where he could warn the agents on the bottom level to go out and arrest him before he even made it inside.

But so far, there had been no sign of him. And as Andre checked in for what felt like the thousandth time, but was actually only every thirty minutes, the other teams confirmed it. Either Keane wasn't here yet, he wasn't taking the bait or he was waiting.

But waiting for what? With every minute he stuck around, the greater the chances were he'd get caught. As someone with a decade in law enforcement, Keane had to know that. If he wanted to come for Juliette—and Andre was sure he did—he had to come soon.

Right now, Andre was wishing for Scott on the scope beside him. With two of them, one could be constantly scanning while the other stayed focused on one spot. With Juliette already so well protected, it wasn't really necessary, but maybe that was why his neck was tingling. He felt as though he was missing something. He never ran missions without his partner.

Andre shifted, settling into his position more fully. He was prone on the ground, his elbows up underneath him to give him a little height. The rifle was lined up at the bottom of the big open space that would become a window, resting just above the sill. It gave him a perfect vantage point, while allowing him the most invisibility. Someone would need to be above him to spot him, and Andre had been watching the roofline of Juliette's building, too, just in case Keane was a daredevil or getting creative.

"We've got a possible," a member of Porter's team came on the radio.

Andre's pulse kicked up slightly. It would have skyrocketed if he wasn't well trained. To take an accurate shot on the rifle, everything needed to be calm and steady: pulse, breathing, hands. "Where?"

"Coming around from the west side of the building now. He should be in your line of sight soon. A male approximately Keane's height and weight. He's wearing a ball cap pulled low and a bulky coat. It's hard to see his face."

"Got him," Andre said, dialing in closer on the scope. It might be hard for the ground agents to get a match, but Andre could get close enough to see the guy's nose hairs if he wanted. Just as soon as the man tilted his head up.

He was walking briskly, heading for the back door of Juliette's apartment building, both hands in his pockets.

"Watch the hands," Andre warned. "He might have a weapon."

The man kept walking, closer and closer to the door of the building until Andre knew he was going to have to tell agents inside to grab him soon. But he didn't want to do it if it wasn't Keane, because that could scare him off.

"Come on, look up," Andre muttered, dialing in even closer. But all he could see was the guy's jaw. It wasn't enough. He took a step even closer to the door and Andre got ready to key his mic when a creak behind him made goose bumps instantly rise on his arms.

He started to spin around, but he wasn't fast enough to stop the butt of a gun from slamming down on his head. Pain exploded and then he crashed onto his rifle.

A man swam in front of Andre's wavering vision and an angry voice snarled, "You shouldn't go after someone else's wife."

Then the stock of the gun crashed down once more and everything went black.

Chapter Nineteen

"Something's wrong." Juliette wasn't sure how she knew it, but a feeling of dread hit her and wouldn't let go.

"You're okay," Marcos said in a stage whisper, breaking the plan not to speak, probably because of the terror in her voice. "They stopped the man just inside the apartment building. It wasn't Keane. He seemed a little more nervous about the whole thing than he should have, so agents are questioning him just in case."

"You think Dylan would have sent someone else after me, instead of coming himself?"

"No," Cole said calmly. "But maybe this guy was a distraction. The agents are on alert." Then his voice got quieter and she knew he was on the radio when he said, "What's Andre's status?"

Juliette strained to hear the answer, finally leaving the couch and standing in the door to her bedroom as the reply came back: "He went offline. We think his radio died. But he's only been off for a minute. I'm sure he'll come back. I've had this happen before with the radios."

"Someone should check on him," Juliette said.

"If he doesn't come back in a few minutes, we will," Cole replied. "He's right. If the radio went off, it should come back. Or Andre will call."

"Let's just call him." She knew it was ridiculous, but something about this felt wrong.

"He's okay," Marcos spoke up. "I just got a text from him. He says his radio died on him, the guy downstairs isn't Dylan, and he'll call if he spots anything."

Juliette let out a heavy breath. "Sorry."

"It's okay," Cole said. "This is stressful. Just try to act normal, okay? There's a pretty small chance he can see you, but we don't want it to be obvious you're talking to anyone. Especially if this guy we just stopped was a decoy."

She must have looked perplexed, because Cole explained, "A distraction. Or a test, to see if the place was being watched. Agents grabbed him inside, so hopefully if Keane is watching outside, everything will seem fine to him. But it could mean he's here." He tapped the radio again. "Let us know when you have word on the man you're questioning."

Twenty-five minutes later, the radio went on and Juliette stood, walking into her bedroom so she could hear the news.

"Someone gave the guy we stopped a hundred bucks to put on a ball cap and keep it low, his head down and hands in pockets, and walk to the back of the apartment building at exactly the time he did. The description of the person who paid him matches Keane. He's nearby."

She was already jumpy, but her nerves increased so much her hands started to shake. She shoved them into the pockets of her borrowed pants and tried to appear unaffected.

"It's going to be fine," Cole promised. "We won't let him get anywhere near you."

So much for nonchalant. She nodded her thanks as Marcos said, "I'm going to text Andre, let him know."

A minute later, Marcos muttered, "This makes no sense."

"I don't know what that is," Cole said. "An autocorrect error?"

Juliette got off the couch and went into the bedroom. "What's happening? Did Andre spot him?"

"I think he's too focused on the scope. His message makes no sense, maybe something weird with autocorrect. Hang on."

"What does it say?"

Marcos jumped to his feet and let out a string of curses, then yanked up his radio and barked, "Someone get to the building across the street, now! Trace my brother's phone. Hurry! Keane has him."

"What?" Juliette grabbed the door frame as her whole world seemed to tilt.

Vaguely, she felt Cole grab her shoulders, as if he was afraid she was going to fall, and then lead her to sit on the bed. She blinked a few times, bringing everything back into focus even as her heart thumped a terrified beat. "How is that possible? Dylan can't have Andre."

"I got a picture from my brother's phone," Marcos said. "Someone else sent it."

Cole was already back on the radio and peering out the window across the street. "Hurry!"

"We should join them," Marcos said, heading for the door.

Cole grabbed him. "We stay here. What if Keane hired someone to help him? He could be trying to draw away Juliette's protection to get her while everyone is distracted."

Juliette jumped to her feet. "Who cares? Go find Andre! Let Dylan come for me. Just make sure Andre is okay!"

Marcos's jaw bunched, but he nodded at Cole. The brothers seemed to come to a silent agreement. Marcos drew his weapon, his expression more fierce than she was used to with his easygoing, teasing grins. "Let's get her out of here."

"No," Cole argued. "We wait for the agents to check on Andre, then move with security around us." He studied Marcos's phone. "That picture was taken in the back of a car. Our best bet is to trace Andre's phone."

"What picture?" Juliette demanded, yanking the phone out of Marcos's hand, even as he tried to pull it back.

She gasped as she got a glimpse of it. The image showed Andre, his eyes closed and his head bent at an awkward angle, bound on what had to be the bench seat in a vehicle. There was blood on his scalp from a nasty gash.

Tears gathered in her eyes until she could barely see the picture. "Is he dead?"

She wasn't even sure the words had passed her lips until Cole said, "No. He's tied up, Juliette. He's just unconscious."

As the phone beeped once more, Marcos swore. "Well, he's not coming here. Keane wants to make a trade."

Juliette blinked the tears back, swiping a hand across her cheeks in case any had gotten free. "Me for Andre," she realized.

"Don't worry—" Cole started.

"Do it," she insisted. "Make the trade."

HIS HEAD WAS killing him. It throbbed with every beat of his heart, and nausea rolled in his stomach, until he knew it was a real possibility he was going to throw up. Except that there was a gag over his mouth and if he threw up, he might choke to death.

Andre focused on breathing in and out through his nose, slowly, until the nausea lessened. He cracked open his eyes, and flashes of light danced in front of him. Beyond that, he could see…something.

He squeezed his eyes shut again and tried to move his hand up to his head, but that just sent pain through his wrists. His hands were trussed behind his back, locked at the wrist by what had to be a zip tie. Slowly, what had happened came back to him: the sudden realization someone was behind him in the empty building. Turning around, but not fast enough. The blow to the head. The furious voice of a man who'd come unhinged. Keane.

Andre opened his eyes again, forcing them not to close against the painful light, until the world around him started to come into focus. He was in a dingy hotel room, lying on his side on disgusting carpeting. A radiator rattled noisily in the corner and a bed was in sight. Off in the distance, he saw a door, presumably to a bathroom.

It was the kind of place you paid for by the

hour. Only people who were desperate or wanting to pay in cash and stay out of sight would visit. Since Keane was a cop, Andre doubted there was anyone within screaming distance. Or if there was, they wouldn't care.

The bathroom door opened and then a pair of work boots strode toward him and stopped. Andre looked up.

Dylan Keane was stocky and muscular, with dark blond hair and eyes the color of an angry storm. He was obviously strong, if he'd carried Andre down three flights of stairs and then into this place. Or—from the achiness all over Andre's back and legs—he'd been dragged part of the way. Dylan might have been attractive at one time, but the stress of having everyone learn his true character was written all over his face.

The other thing written plainly on his face was fury. And it was directed right at Andre.

He sensed the kick coming before Keane drew back his foot and slammed it into his ribs, but with nowhere to go, bracing didn't help much. Andre's head throbbed even more, and the nausea returned, but he tried not to let Keane see how badly it hurt.

From the smirk on Keane's face, he wasn't successful. "You make it a habit of chasing after other men's wives?"

Andre wanted to tell him the fact that Juliette

had run from him for three years should tell him something, but he could barely even move his mouth with the rag shoved in it.

"Don't worry," Keane said. "You won't have to wait long to see her. I've told her how to find me. We'll see her soon. And then it's bye-bye, Mr. FBI."

JULIETTE REMEMBERED SITTING at a diner with Dylan maybe six months into their marriage. She'd been going on and on about an exhibit she'd seen at the art museum, talking about all the different artists. She recalled the flush of excitement from knowing the gallery next to the museum was going to take one of her paintings. She thought Dylan had been excited for her.

Then, all of a sudden, he'd exclaimed, "Renoir! That's it."

"What?" she'd asked.

"That will be our code word for danger."

She'd stared back at him, uncomprehending and frustrated, and then he'd explained, "If there's ever any kind of danger and I need you to get up and get out, no questions asked, I'll say that. Renoir. No one would use it in regular conversation, so it will be perfect."

"*I* was just using it in regular conversation," she'd reminded him. "I was telling you—"

"Just remember the code, Juliette," he'd cut

her off. "If I ever say Renoir, you get up and go. No explanation, nothing. Just do it."

"Juliette," Cole said now, and from his tone she knew he'd been saying her name repeatedly.

She snapped herself out of the memory and focused on his face. "What?"

"What does this mean to you?" He held Marcos's phone up again, this time scrolled back to the text that Marcos had said didn't make any sense:

Renoir. 3A. At the Grind.

He wasn't showing her the last message that had come in after the picture of Andre, but she'd seen it earlier:

Send Juliette alone or Andre is dead.

"Uh, I don't know," she said, but from the expression on his face, Cole was suspicious.

The fact was, she didn't know. Not for sure. But she suspected. *Renoir* meant get out, get away from the agents. *3A* had to mean 3:00 a.m. Dylan had often only used the first letter when jotting down times for things. *The Grind* was what he'd always called his job, and it was the only part she wasn't sure about.

His work was back in Pennsylvania. She doubted he was sending her to a police station nearby. He must mean her work, she realized. The marketing company would be empty at 3:00 a.m.

Her life for Andre's. It was a trade she was willing to make.

"Renoir was his code for danger," she told them, because she knew they wouldn't believe that she didn't understand any of it. "But I don't know about the rest of it."

"Is there a location called The Grind?" Marcos asked. "Maybe a coffee shop?"

"We can look it up," Cole said, still staring at her questioningly.

She tried to keep her expression confused and upset, which wasn't too difficult, and eventually he must have bought it, because he got to his feet and spoke into the radio, telling everyone they were changing locations.

They took her to Shaye's house to hide, because she was far enough outside the loop they didn't think anyone could track her there. While Shaye tried to distract her, Cole and Marcos huddled in the kitchen on a multihour call with the case agents. They had tracked Andre's phone only to find it discarded on the side of the road.

Juliette heard them realize that *3A* was probably 3:00 a.m., but they were having no luck with *The Grind.* Apparently, there were at least three locations within a thirty-mile radius with those words in the title.

"He's going to be okay," Shaye reassured her

now, and Juliette resisted glancing at her watch, knowing it was just after one.

The past few hours had been a jumble of fear and second-guessing herself, but she knew she couldn't risk deviating from what Dylan wanted. Not with Andre's life on the line.

Juliette refocused, staring at the woman across from her who'd opened her home and shared her clothes. Shaye Mallory was tall and thin, which Juliette could have guessed from the fit of her clothes. She had long, curly red hair that didn't seem to want to stay in a clip, and deep brown eyes filled with compassion.

When they'd arrived, Shaye had looked at Cole with barely concealed adoration and embarrassment. There was a story with those two, and Juliette prayed one day, not long from now, they'd have Andre back and she'd get to hear it.

Juliette gave her a shaky smile. "I hope so."

"Maybe you should try to get some sleep," Shaye suggested.

Juliette tried not to look too happy. She'd been hoping for the last twenty minutes that Shaye would suggest that. "I probably should. Wake me if anything happens, okay?"

"Of course." On the way out of the room, Shaye flipped off the overhead light, just leaving on the lamp.

Juliette waited a few minutes after she'd gone

before she stuffed pillows under the covers. She changed into something from Shaye's closet, tossing the clothes she'd been wearing over the end of the bed. She hoped if anyone came in to check on her that it would be enough to fool them. She turned off the lamp, plunging the room into darkness.

Her heart racing, she carefully slid the window open, inch by inch, praying it wouldn't squeak. She had no idea how long it would take her to get to work on foot, or if she'd be able to hitch-hike once she got far enough out from Shaye's house. All she knew was that she couldn't let anyone catch her.

Cole and Marcos were well trained, but so was her ex-husband. And he meant what he said. If she didn't come alone, she had no doubt he'd kill Andre.

She knew she was doing the right thing as she climbed out the window, closing it again behind her. Then she started to run.

Dylan had kidnapped Andre almost six hours ago. What had Dylan done to him in that time?

That worry propelled her on foot until she was panting and a cramp shot through her side. The calf that had been pelted with bits of concrete a few days ago ached. But none of it mattered, because a truck was coming. She jumped out in front of it, waving her arms.

The vehicle slammed to a stop and the man in the driver's seat rolled down his window. "Are you crazy, lady?"

"I need a ride," she gasped. "Please. It's an emergency."

He stared at her a minute longer, probably trying to decide if she really was crazy, then reached over and opened the passenger door. "Get in."

Ten minutes later, after she'd directed him to her old office, he stopped outside the front door, clearly skeptical. "It's closed. Are you sure this is where you need to be?"

"Yes. Thank you for the ride." She jumped out of the truck, glancing around, searching for any sign of Dylan. But everything was dark and empty, almost spooky.

"You want me to wait in case you need a ride back?" the man persisted.

"No," she snapped. She needed him to leave, so Dylan didn't think she'd brought backup. Why hadn't she asked him to drop her down the street? "Sorry. I'm fine. Please go."

He shook his head, muttering something under his breath, but he drove off, leaving her all alone.

And she sure felt alone. She crossed her arms over her chest, cold as she looked around, from the dark building and empty parking lot to the woods out behind the office where a hit man had dragged her, intending to keep her as leverage before putting a bullet in her head.

A car raced around the corner, then slammed to a stop in front of her so fast it made her jump backward.

A tinted window rolled down on the passenger's side and Dylan glared back at her from his place behind the wheel. His furious expression was ten times worse than when he'd scared her enough to send her running for her life three years ago.

She resisted the urge to take another step backward.

"Get in."

"Let Andre go and then I will," she replied. Her voice only shook a little bit.

"You get in the car in the next five seconds or I shoot Andre in the head," Dylan barked.

Juliette got in the car, and it shot backward out of the parking lot so fast she slammed into the dashboard. Grabbing it for support, she looked in the backseat. It was empty.

The car did a three-point turn fast enough to make her head spin, then raced away from her office.

Chapter Twenty

"Guess who I found," Keane announced.

Andre stopped his useless attempts to free his hands and looked up just in time to see Keane shove Juliette toward him, hard enough that she hit the bed and bounced off the edge, then landed on the ground beside him.

In his mind, he screamed her name, but he still couldn't make a sound with the gag in his mouth. Keane had insisted he was going for a drive and that he'd be back with Juliette, but Andre hadn't believed it. How had she gotten away from his brothers? No way would they have let her go alone.

For a second, he hoped they were somewhere behind her, but the sorrowful expression on Juliette's face told him she'd come by herself.

He said a silent prayer that his brothers were tracking her. Wherever Keane had met up with her, it couldn't have been far, because he hadn't been gone more than ten minutes.

Juliette scooted toward him, reaching her hand out to his face, but Keane grabbed her arm and yanked her to her feet, roughly enough that it had to hurt.

Andre tried to yell, but the gag swallowed it. As hard as he'd worked on his binds while Keane was gone, he hadn't been able to get free. He'd managed to push himself against the bed and he'd been sawing the zip tie on the metal frame. But although he was making a small pile of plastic shavings under the bed, it wasn't going fast enough. Not even close.

He'd tried pushing himself to his feet only to discover his ankles were tied together, too, and there was a loop going from his ankles to his wrists. Essentially, he wasn't going anywhere.

How had he let this happen? How had he not considered that Keane would make a grab for him instead of Juliette? Now she was going to pay for caring about him. And how much she cared was written all over her face. His breath caught at the love he saw there, and he willed her to hide it before Keane saw, too.

"You promised you'd let him go," Juliette said, yanking her arm free of her ex's grasp. "I'm here. You have what you want."

Keane smiled at her, and it was so cocky and

full of gloating that Andre wished he could knock it off the man's face with a swift punch. But he couldn't stand, and if he tried to swing a punch, there was a good chance he'd throw up.

"Well, originally, I thought I might," Keane said, and his voice was so full of hate that Andre could hardly believe he'd once been married to her.

He also understood in that instant every hesitation Juliette had ever had about diving into a new relationship.

"But I see how you care about him, and I think I'll hold on to him a little longer."

Juliette instantly blanked her face, but Keane just laughed, then leaned close so they were nose to nose and whispered, "I know you too well."

For a second, she seemed to be considering fighting him and then Keane pulled a gun from his waistband and shook it at her. He took a step back and sank into a chair. "Go ahead. Take a seat. Let's chat."

Juliette seemed wary as she glanced from him to Keane, but then she sat gingerly on the edge of the bed. "What is there to talk about? You came to kill me? Fine. Do it. But leave Andre out of it."

At her words, Andre redoubled his efforts to break free of the zip ties, but all he succeeded in doing was bloodying his wrists worse than he already had. He'd never felt so helpless in his life.

Juliette sank to her knees next to him. Her eyes were broadcasting all the things she was trying to keep off her face as she untied the gag from around his mouth.

For a second, he thought Keane was going to argue, but he let her do it, then gestured with the gun for her to stand back up.

Free of the gag, Andre's throat felt like he'd gargled sand and his mouth felt like someone had shoved cotton in it, but he managed to rasp, "You think she cares about me? You're wrong. She turned me down because of you. If you hadn't blown it by threatening to kill her, she'd still be with you."

Juliette looked shocked, blinking at him as though she wasn't sure if he actually believed his words or it was some kind of ploy. Keane looked suspicious, then a little hopeful.

Andre prayed it would work. He knew his only chance was that the FBI would track them down in time, and he didn't think it was probable. But Juliette had a shot, because underneath all of Keane's anger and hate was something else. He still loved her, in his own sick, twisted way.

And if they could convince Keane she loved him too, he might let her live.

JULIETTE BIT BACK her instant response to Andre's ridiculous comment. For a second, it had stunned her silent, because she'd thought he really believed it, that he didn't know she loved *him*. But that moment of surprise saved her, because she recognized what he was doing. He was trying to get Keane to keep her alive, no matter what happened to him.

And she realized he was right. Dylan's biggest flaw had always been his own ego. If she could convince him she still loved him, maybe she could find a way to talk him into leaving with her—and keeping Andre alive.

The thought of going anywhere with Dylan gave her chills, but she fought them and did her best to appear embarrassed, as if Andre was right. She wasn't sure Dylan was buying it, but as long as he was talking, he wasn't shooting, so she put as much indignation as she could into her voice as she asked, "Did you send those men after me? Did you really try to kill me? Because I kept your secret all these years."

He frowned at her, glanced down to Andre and then back up, as if he didn't know what game they were playing. He settled the gun on his lap and shrugged. "Sorry, babe. Harkin was freaking out at the idea of you still being out there somewhere, knowing the truth."

"And so you decided you'd kill me instead of dealing with him? He's the murderer!"

"Yeah, well, he was a problem I was planning to take care of, too. I would have, if the FBI hadn't rushed into that house when they did. I'd been in Virginia for days by then, tracking him. It was crappy timing for me when the FBI found him."

His words felt like a sucker punch even though she'd known it had to be him. Still, some part of her had foolishly hoped it was Harkin. And yet... She squinted at Dylan, trying to figure out what about his blasé tone felt wrong to her.

He scowled at Andre. "That really screwed me up. Before you did that, I thought I could go back to work. But I assume he's told all, probably skewing the story to make himself look good, right?"

"He said you harassed him for a payoff on a murder he didn't commit, otherwise you were going to frame him."

Dylan snorted. "Oh, he did it. When Jim told Harkin I'd figured out he was the one who framed Loews, he offered to let me in on what he was giving Jim. And yeah, after that, he was fair game. I gave the guy a free pass on murder, so he owed me. But I never threatened to frame him for something he didn't do. That guy was guilty."

His scowl deepened. "And I can't believe you fell for that trick in Leming. I've been here for days. I followed Harkin to Quantico, the idiot.

I would have taken care of him then, but I realized what he was doing and I wanted to find Juliette, too." His gaze shifted back up to her. "I saw you with this *Fed*. You sure seemed cozy."

Juliette recalled that moment when Andre had run up to her at the entrance to Quantico and swept her into his arms, and she'd felt safe again. The fact that Dylan had seen it all made the moment feel slightly tainted.

Andre had taken her to the field office from Quantico, Juliette realized. Dylan must have lost her there and gone back to Harkin's house, then seen the police car nearby and held off on killing Harkin yet again.

"When did you turn into...this?" Juliette asked softly. She knew it blew Andre's plan, but she couldn't keep it up. Dylan was never going to buy that she still loved him unconditionally. Not only had he just admitted he'd tried to have her killed, but as much as she knew his flaws, he knew hers, too. He might have always put her feelings second when they were together, but she hadn't sat silently in the background. She'd spoken her opinion.

Dylan leaned toward her, his hands gripping the edges of the chair as though he'd forgotten the gun was in his lap. "You know how awful it is, being a patrol cop? Even a detective? Dealing day in and day out with these civilians who call you names, who you have to worry will pull a gun on you because you want to give them a speeding ticket? Being a detective was worse, like wading into the scum of the earth. Jerks like Harkin were out there getting rich, and I was barely paying the mortgage risking my life for them. I deserved some of that."

How had she not seen this? She stared at him now, barely recognizing the man she'd fallen in love with so many years ago.

He scoffed at her, leaning back in his seat. "You still love me, huh? If you want to play that card, you might want to wipe the look of disgust off your face, babe."

"Don't call me that," she snapped, standing up and striding toward him.

He lifted the gun, pointing it at her. "Uh-uh. Don't get a backbone now."

"What are we doing here, Dylan? What's the point of this?" She could practically hear Andre behind her, telling her not to antagonize him, but she couldn't stop.

All those times Dylan had caught up to her over the years came back to her in flashes of memories. He probably could have killed her any of those times. But he hadn't. Instead, he'd sent hit men after her, and staring into his eyes now, she knew why.

He could take a bribe from a murderer, he

could even pay off criminals to kill his ex-wife, but he couldn't do it himself. She might have been playing a ruse, but he was, too. On some level, *he* still loved *her*.

She stood right in front of him, making sure her body blocked Andre from the gun, the way he'd taught her to stand in the apartment. Only this time it was backward, not giving Dylan an angle.

He got slowly to his feet, and for a terrifying instant, she thought she'd misjudged him. But then he set the gun beside him on the arm of the chair and reached up, gripping her upper arms hard enough to bruise. "I haven't really decided yet. I guess it's up to you whether I take you with me or kill you here." His voice turned careless. "Your boyfriend, though? He's dead either way."

He dropped her arms and lifted his eyebrows, as if he was waiting for an answer.

She moved fast, grabbing the gun off the chair, and jerked herself backward. She practically fell onto the bed as she dove out of range before she turned it around and got her finger under the trigger guard.

Dylan gave her a smirk as he pulled a switchblade from his pocket and flipped it open. "That wasn't a good idea." He took a step toward her.

"Don't move," she barked, her voice almost as shaky as her hands. She hated guns. She'd always hated even holding them, but Dylan had taught her to shoot. He knew she could hit a target, but he also knew a target was all she'd ever been willing to hit, no matter how many what-if scenarios he'd thrown at her. She'd told him she didn't think she'd be able to shoot another person if her life depended on it.

He took a step toward her.

Out of the corner of her eye, she saw Andre jerking around on the ground, trying to gain purchase to rush him.

"I know you, Juliette. You can't shoot me."

"You don't know me anymore," she swore, but her hands were still shaking, and she knew he was right. She couldn't shoot him. Not even to save her own life.

Dylan's smile grew and then his attention shifted to Andre on the ground. And in that instant, she saw his intent: after he disarmed her, he *would* kill Andre.

Juliette pulled the trigger.

Dylan fell backward but didn't hit the ground. It was as though he was on drugs. He roared when the bullet hit, then rushed toward her, his arm dripping blood.

She fumbled to fire again, but he was almost on her, the knife outstretched, and she panicked, twisting to get away.

Then, suddenly, Dylan went down, toppling to the ground, away from her.

For a second, Juliette didn't know what had happened. Then she realized that Andre had somehow managed to get up on his knees and tackle Dylan. The two of them were on the ground, locked together so Juliette knew she couldn't shoot.

Dylan's hands were on Andre's throat and his hands and feet were still tied behind him.

The knife had fallen somewhere, but Juliette didn't waste time trying to find it. Instead, she dropped the gun and leaped on top of her ex-husband, wrenching his hands away from Andre's neck, tears in her eyes as she heard Andre gasping for breath.

Then Dylan flipped her over, climbing on top of her, the fury on his face more horrifying than when he'd threatened to kill her, and she wished her hands hadn't shaken at the exact wrong time, sending that bullet wide.

His hands went for her throat and she grabbed his wrists, trying to hold him off, but he was stronger and slowly he pushed back, even with his injured arm. Her arms started to tremble with the effort and then he got them over her head, pinning both of her hands with one of his.

She kneed him in the groin with all her

strength and he fell forward with a yelp. She didn't waste time, shooting her hand out and hitting as hard as she could right on his injury. He fell backward, but before she could move, he was coming for her again.

Then, all of a sudden, he flew off her and Andre was there, blood dripping down both of his hands, the zip tie gone. His feet were still bound, though, and Dylan was coming back.

Andre turned, lifting his arms in a boxer's pose, but she could tell he was unsteady on his feet, and Dylan was enraged, racing back for more.

Juliette tried to push to her feet and then she saw it: Dylan's gun, on the ground beside her. She grabbed it, gripping it with hands that barely shook now. "Don't move or I swear this time I'll aim for your heart."

Dylan froze and she could see him trying to figure out if she'd really shot to wound last time or if she was bluffing. Before he could decide, Andre's fist darted out, landing solidly in the center of Dylan's face. He fell to the ground, out cold.

For a minute, Juliette watched him, sure he'd get back up. Then she looked at Andre, swaying on his feet but still willing to stand in front of her, and she set the gun on the bed and took a step forward. She wanted to stand beside him now.

"It's over," he told her.

"I love you," she replied, then kissed him.

Epilogue

Three weeks later, Juliette stood on the front porch of her brand-new house. It was a rental, but it was a step toward permanency. She'd decorated inside with so many pieces of artwork that Andre called it her own private gallery. He joked that she should sell tickets for a tour of her house.

He'd let her put up paintings in his house, too, which was good, because as much as she liked her new house—and her new job at a gallery in DC that Shaye had helped her find—she spent more time at Andre's house. She loved the artwork, loved the sense of having something that was hers, but her favorite thing about Andre's home were his photos. She'd been working on adding more personal photos to her place, too.

"What are you thinking about?" Andre asked,

coming up behind her and wrapping his arms around her waist.

She leaned against him, her head fitting perfectly underneath his chin. "The future."

She'd finally put the past behind her. It would always be a part of her, but her life was no longer in a holding pattern.

The Manning case had been officially reopened and Loews had been released from jail after Harkin had finally confirmed that Loews was innocent. Both Dylan and Harkin were in prison awaiting trial, and the FBI had assured her neither one would ever be getting out. Not long ago, that would have caused her some heartache, knowing the man she'd once pledged her love to was enduring a life in prison. Now, she'd learned to accept that Dylan had made his own choices and she was free to make hers.

She still had moments of panic about being in a new relationship, about trusting someone enough to let him into her heart. But Andre had managed to sneak in there despite her best defenses, and she was glad.

"What about the future?" Andre asked.

She spun in his embrace, looping her arms around his neck as she stared up at him. "I'm glad it's going to be with you."

He smiled down at her, and she could barely

see the stitches on his head anymore. "Me, too. Have I told you lately that I love you?"

She pretended to consider it. "Not for the last hour or so, at least."

"I better remedy that," he whispered, then pulled her even closer and pressed his lips to hers.

She went up on her tiptoes to kiss him more deeply, loving the feel of his heart thumping wildly against her.

After a minute, he pulled back to whisper, "I did promise to kiss you good-night on your front porch someday."

She grinned. It was a promise he'd been keeping every day since she moved in. "Good night?"

He smiled back and then she squealed as he scooped her into his arms. "Well, time for bed, anyway."

The dimple that popped on his left cheek made her skin tingle. But staring up into his eyes, full of all the things she'd seen on that first day he'd swept into her life—the goodness, the honesty, the protectiveness—she got serious. Palming his cheek, she told him, "I love you. I want you to kiss me on this porch every night for the rest of our lives."

His smile turned soft and tender. "That promise will be easy to keep."

"I'm ready for a new life, Andre. And I want it to be with you."

Andre pushed the door open with his shoulder. "Then, let's start right now," he said, striding inside. Toward their future. Together.

* * * * *

Don't miss the next book in
THE LAWMEN: BULLETS AND BRAWN,
POLICE PROTECTOR

And check out previous titles in
THE LAWMEN *series:*

DISARMING DETECTIVE
SEDUCED BY THE SNIPER
SWAT SECRET ADMIRER

Available now from Harlequin Intrigue!

Get 2 Free Books,
Plus 2 Free Gifts—
just for trying the Reader Service!

HARLEQUIN *Presents*

Get 2 Free Books,
Plus 2 Free Gifts—
just for trying the
Reader Service!

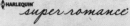

HOMETOWN HEARTS ♥

YES! Please send me **The Hometown Hearts Collection** in Larger Print. This collection begins with 3 FREE books and 2 FREE gifts in the first shipment. Along with my 3 free books, I'll also get the next 4 books from the Hometown Hearts Collection, in LARGER PRINT, which I may either return and owe nothing, or keep for the low price of $4.99 U.S./ $5.89 CDN each plus $2.99 for shipping and handling per shipment*. If I decide to continue, about once a month for 8 months I will get 6 or 7 more books, but will only need to pay for 4. That means 2 or 3 books in every shipment will be FREE! If I decide to keep the entire collection, I'll have paid for only 32 books because 19 books are FREE! I understand that accepting the 3 free books and gifts places me under no obligation to buy anything. I can always return a shipment and cancel at any time. My free books and gifts are mine to keep no matter what I decide.

262 HCN 3432 462 HCN 3432

Name	(PLEASE PRINT)	
Address		Apt. #
City	State/Prov.	Zip/Postal Code

Signature (if under 18, a parent or guardian must sign)

Mail to the **Reader Service:**
IN U.S.A.: P.O. Box 1867, Buffalo, NY. 14240-1867
IN CANADA: P.O. Box 609, Fort Erie, Ontario L2A 5X3

* Terms and prices subject to change without notice. Prices do not include applicable taxes. Sales tax applicable in NY. Canadian residents will be charged applicable taxes. This offer is limited to one order per household. All orders subject to approval. Credit or debit balances in a customer's account(s) may be offset by any other outstanding balance owed by or to the customer. Please allow 4 to 6 weeks for delivery. Offer available while quantities last. Offer not available to Quebec residents.